SUMMER

of the

Gypsy

Moths

SUMMER
of the
Gypsy
Moths

SARA PENNYPACKER

BALZER + BRAY
An Imprint of HarperCollins*Publishers*

Balzer + Bray is an imprint of HarperCollins Publishers.

Summer of the Gypsy Moths

Library of Congress Cataloging-in-Publication Data
Pennypacker, Sara, date
The summer of the gypsy moths / Sara Pennypacker. — 1st ed.
    p.   cm.
Summary: A foster child named Angel and twelve-year-old Stella, who are living
with Stella's great-aunt Louise at a cottage colony on Cape Cod, secretly assume
responsibility for the vacation rentals when Louise unexpectedly dies and the girls
are afraid of being returned to the foster care system.
ISBN 978-0-06-196422-0
    [1. Secrets—Fiction.   2. Loss (Psychology)—Fiction.   3. Great aunts—Fiction.
4. Death—Fiction.   5. Cape Cod (Mass.)—Fiction.]   I. Title.
PZ7.P3856Su 2012   2011026095
[Fic]—dc23   CIP
                                                                        AC

Typography by Sarah Hoy
17 18 BVG 10 9 8 7 6
❖
First paperback edition, 2013

*To the Virginia Center for the Creative Arts,
where this book was born*

SUMMER
of the
Gypsy
Moths

CHAPTER 1

The earth spins at a thousand miles an hour. Sometimes when I remember this, it's all I can do to stay upright—the urge to flatten myself to the ground and clutch hold is that strong. Because, gravity? Oh, gravity is no match for a force that equals ten simultaneous hurricanes. No, if we aren't all flung off the earth like so many water droplets off a cartoon dog's back, it must be because people are connected somehow. I like to imagine the ties between us as strands of spider silk: practically invisible, maybe, but strong as steel. I figure the trick is to spin out enough of them to weave ourselves into a net.

Discovering one of these ties feels so good—as if I'm settling more safely into the earth, as if my bones are made of iron and my blood is melted lead. Because I never know when I'm going to find one, I'm always on the lookout. The whole time I lived with Louise, I was watching.

Finally, on the last day of her life—in the last hour before she died, most likely—I found one. Actually, Louise found it. She threw it out like a lifeline. I grabbed.

"Fix yourself some breakfast, then help me unload the car, Stella. I went down to the Agway yesterday, got some fertilizer and mulch for my blueberries."

"I love blueberries," I said. "So does my mom." I pulled a box of pancakes out of the freezer and braced for the sarcastic remark about my mother I figured was coming.

Louise grabbed the box and clattered the last two pancakes onto a plate. "Puh," she muttered. Puh, I'd noticed, was the start of a lot of her conversations. As though she'd taken in a mouthful of road dust and had to spit it out before she could form any words.

"Puh," she started again. "You're telling me. That girl was crazy for blueberries." She winced when she realized what she'd said, and frowned over at me to see if she had to apologize. But I didn't react. My mother wasn't crazy. That wasn't it.

"What I mean is, she was always hounding me to buy 'em. Course, they cost an arm and a leg out of season; I didn't have enough money to go buying 'em whenever she got a whim." She shoved the plate into the microwave and stabbed the Start button extra hard, to show me how she felt about things. Then she stopped. She pushed aside the curtains over the sink to gaze out the window, and when she turned back, her face had softened to almost pretty. For the first time, I could see how she and my grandmother could have been sisters.

"Out there," she said. "Past the garden. You see those bushes?"

I stepped beside her and nodded. I saw bushes—twenty or thirty at least. They didn't impress me much, I have to say.

"Your mother helped me plant 'em. Because she loved 'em so much. Couldn't have been more than eight or nine, but she worked like a little trouper. Never quit. Three different highbush varieties. I got Pipkins for muffins. . . ."

I stopped listening for a minute as it hit me again: My mother had lived here. Right. Exactly. Here. Louise had taken in my grandmother and my mom—her sister and her niece—when my grandmother's husband left. "Supposed to be just until they got on their feet. Turned into two years," Louise had said. "Your mother was a handful even then. It was a long two years."

I looked around, wondering if she had eaten from these dishes, sat in these chairs. I'd been poking around whenever I could but hadn't found any trace of her yet. It was as if Louise had scrubbed her away, the way she scrubbed her kitchen every morning.

The microwave dinged, but Louise was on a roll. ". . . Northern Beauties for pies," she was saying. "I'm known for my pies—you ask anyone." She tapped a cluster of photos taped to the refrigerator—pies with blue ribbons hanging next to them. "First prize, four years running. Woulda taken it last year, too, if Ellen Rogers hadn't married herself a judge. No matter—I bring my pies down to the diner, word gets out, the line stretches past the drugstore. George Nickerson would walk a mile on his knees for a slice. Folks think the secret to a great pie is the crust, but no, it's the berries. Store-bought taste like paste. I grow 'em myself, leave 'em set till they're ripe, blue all the way round."

"That's how I like them, too. No green," I said. "They look like blue pearls to me, like something a princess in a fairy tale would make a magic necklace out of."

I didn't tell her the rest: that when I was seven, I had taken a needle and thread and strung my mother a blueberry necklace for her birthday. She'd worn it all day, and

4

even though it stained her blouse, she'd said it made her feel enchanted. And of course I didn't tell her what had happened that night.

"Puh! I don't know about any magic necklaces," Louise said. Then she turned and looked at me as if she was seeing me for the first time, even though I'd been living there for almost two months. "But I'll tell you what. If the gypsy moths don't get those bushes, there'll be berries come August. You help me do the work this summer—and it's a lot of work, tending those bushes, I won't kid you—you help me, and then you get yourself up early enough to beat the birds to pick 'em, and I'll teach you how to make a pie. How's that?" She raised her arms and lurched toward me, then wrapped herself around my shoulders. She pulled away and looked down at her arms as if the hug had been as big a surprise to her as it was to me. She cinched her faded green robe tighter. "I mean, if you want to," she said. "Puh."

She turned away to look out at the garden again. "Which reminds me." She glanced up at the kitchen clock. "Plenty of time before the bus comes. You want berries in August, you come out and help me for five minutes now."

The microwave dinged again then, but Louise had already scuffed out, the screen door banging her on the butt. She wasn't exactly a fast mover. I followed and paused on the step. My mother had stood right here twenty summers ago, looking over this same backyard, the same blue water in the distance. The June sunshine prickled my shoulders through my T-shirt, and it occurred to me: My great-aunt had just hugged me. First time.

She popped the trunk on her rusty white Escort. "You gonna just stand there all day, grinning like an idiot? These sacks aren't gonna grow legs."

Together we hoisted the forty-pound bags of pine bark and fertilizer from the trunk and dragged them one by one to the back of the garden. Seeing her huffing and groaning from the effort, I had an inspiration. As we dropped the last bag, I said, "My mother's still a great worker—really strong. Once she built this altar thing out of rocks, dragged them all home by herself. She never quit!" Well, until the police came and made her return the rocks, claiming some rule about town property. I kept that part to myself, of course. I nodded over to the cottage colony next door. "It's probably a lot of hard work, being the manager," I said, all casual. "If my mom lived here, she and I could do all the heavy work for you like nothing. Wouldn't that be great?"

Louise gave another road-dust "Puh!" and rasped in a few breaths with her hand to her chest. "Well," she admitted, wiping away some hair that had gotten plastered to her sweaty forehead, "having a little help around this place would certainly be a welcome change." As if I weren't right there, heaving those bags around with her!

I jumped on the opening. "She'd settle down here, I know it. She was good when we lived with Gram. Just until she gets on her feet—"

Louise put up a hand. "Don't start, Stella. Too much water under that bridge."

That was how she ended every conversation about my mother. The funny thing was, my mother had always used the same phrase when I'd asked about Louise. "Why don't we see her? Why don't I know her?" Too much water under that bridge.

"Anyway," Louise was saying, "last I checked, we've got a full house as it is."

Angel. I followed Louise back inside, feeling the day cloud over.

CHAPTER

◇ 2 ◇

"Hey, those were mine!"

Angel hung over the sink, pouring syrup over a folded pancake. She eyed me through her hair and took a bite, then tossed the rest of it into the trash and stalked out.

I stayed cool, remembering the Museum of Science film about icebergs I'd seen. Those icebergs, floating silent and steady, ignoring the fierce storms raging around them. Since Angel had moved in, I'd had to remind myself about the icebergs a lot.

I washed my hands, then dug a granola bar out of the cupboard and ate it. Beside me, Louise shook out two lunch bags and slid a banana into each. When she began slapping together some tuna sandwiches, I got two bottles of water from the freezer. "Because of the mayonnaise and salmonella," I reminded her helpfully. "I learned about it in one of Heloise's hints. Also—"

From the living room, I heard Angel snort. She snorted every time I mentioned Heloise, which just went to show what kind of a person she was, since Heloise does nothing but good for people with her household hints column, helping them get their lives in order.

I ignored it, still in iceberg mode. "Also, frozen juice boxes are good." I zipped one of the lunch bags into my backpack and gathered my stuff. "Well, I guess I'll go."

I paused, wondering if the hug had been some kind of signal that things had changed, and we were now the kind of relatives who went around hugging each other. I wasn't sure I wanted that. But I wasn't sure that I didn't, either. I took a step back toward Louise and raised my arms, smiling.

She looked up from pouring her coffee. "Off with you, then," she said.

"Right," I said. "See you."

I went out and settled myself on the split-rail fence in front of the house. It wasn't time for the bus, but the strategy I had developed with Angel was this: Wherever she was, I wasn't. Most days, "Pass the ketchup" was about the limit of our conversation.

"Oil and water" was how Louise saw it. "Puh. I take in a foster kid to keep you company, and don't you two turn out to be oil and water."

Which wasn't fair. First of all, I'd reminded Louise I was almost twelve, not some kindergartener who needed a playmate. She wouldn't give in, though. "You're going to get lonely, especially once summer starts and I get busy with the cottages," she insisted. When Angel had first gotten here, a couple of weeks ago, I had tried, I really had. It's just hard to be friendly to a cactus. Angel was all spines.

"Your heart's like any other muscle, Stella," my grandmother would have said if she'd been here. "You have to stretch it out when it cramps up."

I bent down to brush aside some pebbles in front of an ant that was struggling under a huge load. All right, then, Angel's had it tough, I reminded myself. Maybe if I were an orphan, I'd act like some Dark Queen of All Tragedy, too, the way she did—as if she were the only person in the world who'd ever had anything rotten happen to her, and everyone else had better stay out of her way.

I tried again to find a single real connection between Angel and me. We were both in sixth grade, living under the same roof and all, but those were just coincidences of geography and timing. There were no real ties between us.

But Louise! I hooked my feet under the bottom rail and smiled at the morning's surprise discovery, remembering how she had turned almost pretty when she was telling me about her blueberry bushes—the ones she wanted me to help her with, the ones my mom had helped to plant. A triple tie, it was, linking all three of us together.

I'd tell my mom about it next time she called. Mrs. Marino had warned me not to press her. "She's got a ways to go, Stella," she'd said. "She's got to come back and take the parenting classes. Then she'll have to show improved reliability—a job, a home."

"But it will be by Labor Day. I'm just here for the summer, right?" I'd asked.

"Well, that's the goal, yes," she'd said. "Just don't expect too much, too fast."

I'd agreed, but that didn't mean I couldn't remind my mom of the time she'd lived here where I was now. Of the blueberry bushes she'd planted with Louise. It might be just what she needed—to be reminded of the strands holding her in place. My mom's personal gravity was a little weak.

Just then, Bus Two came rumbling down Pine Lane, kicking up its cloud of sandy dust. At the last second, as usual, Angel came tearing out of the house and raced past me. I followed her to her throne at the very back and sat down. Angel yanked up her backpack, all set to huff away. I stuck my arm out to block her. "I want to talk to you about something. Just for a minute."

Angel tried to shove past me, but I held firm until she scowled and made a big dramatic show of slamming her backpack down. I pictured the banana in her lunch. Angel never ate anything as healthy as a banana, but still, it would be a slimy brown mess by lunchtime. Good, I couldn't help thinking. Serves you right. Another heart cramp.

Angel turned to the window, her hair swinging down like a black curtain between us, and pulled her earphones from her backpack.

"I've been thinking," I started. "It's almost summer, and . . . Angel, will you *listen*?"

Angel started untangling the wires. "Save it. I heard."

"You heard?"

"Windows are open. You want Louise to let your mother live here, and you figure you have a better chance of convincing her if you get me on your side."

"Well," I said, surprised that she'd guessed it so right and feeling a little guilty—as if Angel had caught me at something. Which she hadn't. "Well, so . . . ?"

Angel snapped the earphones over her ears, but then she pushed them back. "What's the matter with her, anyway? Is she . . . ?" Angel circled a forefinger at her temple.

"No. No! She's just . . ." You'd think after living with my mother my whole life, I'd have figured out a way to explain her. But I hadn't. I usually ended up using one of my grandmother's words for her. Flighty. High-strung. "Restless."

Angel rolled her eyes. "They took you away from her because she's *restless*?"

I sighed. "She's had some setbacks lately," I said. Which was true. Gram getting sick and dying. Then having to sell her house to pay the hospital bills. "We're not homeless," my mother would say. "We're house free!" Then she'd chased a string of jobs that didn't work out—people got jealous of my mom's creative talents—and we'd had to move so much. Each place was smaller and crummier than the last, and with each move, my mother had acted a little more . . . "She's just gotten a little off track, that's all. But she'd be fine here. You'd like her. She'd share my room, and we could—"

"A little off track? Louise said someone called the cops on her for *abandoning* you." Angel fished a Dum Dum from her pocket and stuck it into the corner of her mouth.

"That person should have minded her own business," I said, forming the words carefully because it felt like my face had suddenly turned to glass. I studied the gray-shingled houses passing by. My mother hadn't abandoned me. I just hadn't gotten in the car before she left that last time. I should have seen she was getting ready to veer off, and gotten in the car.

I turned back to Angel. "My mom would have come back on her own. She was never gone more than a few days. She'd be fine if she lived here. Just fine. And besides, it would be better for Louise. To have her niece around. I think she's really starting to like having us live with her. Like maybe she wants to make a family—"

Angel yanked the Dum Dum out of her mouth and stabbed it toward me, about an inch from my face. "You are pathetic, Stella, you know that? She *had* to take you in, and the only thing she likes about having me is the check the state sends her."

"She wouldn't be a foster parent for that. Nobody would," I said.

More jabbing with the lollipop. "Seventeen dollars a day. It adds up. Helps her buy all that junk from the Home Shopping Channel."

I closed my eyes and filled my head with icebergs, until I could practically smell the salty fog of their breath. I opened my eyes. "Angel, please. I'm just saying, if Louise mentions about my mom coming, maybe you could—"

"Stella, whatever *Brady Bunch* fantasy you're dreaming up, leave me out of it. I don't care. Besides, I'm not sticking around long enough to be part of it anyway."

That caught me completely by surprise. "You're leaving? When?"

Angel plugged the Dum Dum back in and slid down the window, pulling her hair between us. She thumbed her music on. Disgust waves practically smoked off her.

At the next stop, I got up and moved across the aisle. Angel didn't even turn around, but so what? All through the bus ride, I smiled to myself about the news of that freed-up bedroom. Now maybe my mom really could come to live here. I smiled all through school, too—with only a week left, the teachers had pretty much given up. I smiled and daydreamed about a new life.

In the mornings, after I'd done some chores, I'd head out—to school, or to the beach if it was summer—so my mom could spend the days scrapbooking or sculpting, or whatever her new thing was. She went through phases pretty fast. Anyway, I'd make sure she didn't get stressed out. She'd be so happy, I could stop waking up in the middle of the night to make sure she was still here.

Louise would be happy to have us around, too. In the afternoons, we'd help her with those blueberry bushes, and then maybe we'd watch her soap with her—who knew? Afterward we might get cones at Dairy Queen, or go to a movie or something. We'd do everything that normal families do. By the time I climbed onto the bus home that afternoon, I practically had us picking a puppy from the shelter.

Angel was wrong. It wasn't pathetic to imagine a brand-new life. It was important to stay positive. That was one of the things I admired most about Heloise—no matter what life throws at Heloise, she just cleans it up and looks on the bright side.

Angel missed the bus home as usual, so I knew I had fifteen minutes before she got there. I dumped my backpack inside the front door and then cut around to the backyard. The ground there was sandy and rough, clumped with scratchy-looking bushes. I examined one of them. Sure enough, the twigs were knobbed with tiny berries—hard and green, but still, you could tell they'd be blueberries when they ripened.

I ran into the kitchen. "Hey, want me to weed around those blueberry bushes?" I called out. "Or give them some of that fertilizer?"

And then I stopped. The counter was littered and the cream was still out. Louise was sloppy about herself, but never about her kitchen. The smell of scorched coffee filled the air—the coffee in the carafe had boiled down to a burnt skin. I flipped off the Mr. Coffee. "Louise?" Her name sounded lost in the room, as if it was hanging in the air, looking for something to attach to. "Hey, Louise?"

No answer.

"Don't be a baby, Stella," I told myself out loud. "She just had to go somewhere. People go places all the time." But the back of my neck felt the way alarm bells sound, as if my skin were ringing. It was the feeling I got whenever my mother left me.

I glanced at the clock—in five minutes, Louise's soap would be on. She never missed it. She'd be right back.

I pushed aside the curtains, which she always opened after the *Today* show—always, like it was a rule. I liked that about her—she knew how important it was to keep to a schedule. The Escort was sitting in the driveway. My great-aunt wasn't what you'd call the take-a-walk-for-the-pleasure-of-it type. Even on a beautiful day like today, it would take a flat tire to get her to walk somewhere, and the tires looked okay to me. The bags from Agway were still stacked where we'd left them. Beside the garden gate, a tray of seedlings looked wilted.

I walked into the living room and called louder. "Hey, Louise?"

The alarm bells were drilling up to my scalp now. I've gotten this feeling a lot—if the past two years had been a movie, alarm bells would have been the sound track.

I'm never wrong about this feeling, about what it means.

It's the one skill I've got. Except I had to be wrong now.

I went back into the kitchen, stacked the dishes in the dishwasher, put the cream away, and wiped the counter. Louise's pill dispenser was open, seven compartments full of vitamins that were supposed to keep her looking young. Friday's pills were still there. I snapped the cover down and glanced up at the clock. Nearly three.

I ran water to rinse the coffee carafe. The hot glass tightened with a sharp creak and I jumped. Three o'clock. She should have been stretched out in her recliner by now, a Diet Coke and a stack of Fig Newtons beside her, back-talking the characters.

And that's when I finally heard it: The television was on. I had a second of relief. But what I heard was a woman with a rocks-in-a-bucket voice snarling at someone to "Suck it up, Cupcake." Judge Geraldine.

Not Louise's soap.

I headed for the den to turn it off.

She was there. But she was gone. My knees crashed to the floor.

CHAPTER

3

"Oh, crap!"

I looked up and saw Angel. She dropped her backpack. It thudded with a heaviness it couldn't possibly have carried, like a cinder block.

"Oh, crap," Angel whispered again, staring over me. "*Ô Jesus querido. . . .*"

I followed her gaze. And saw it again.

"Dead person. She's dead. Oh, my God, oh, crap . . . oh, crap . . . dead person."

"Stop saying that," I said. "Something's wrong with her, and—"

"Something's *wrong*? She's dead! Look at her. That's a dead person. Oh, crap . . ."

I reached for the doorway and pulled myself up. My legs felt like they were stuffed with cotton, as if all the bones and muscles had just powdered away. I swayed and gripped the doorway, but my arms were pretty cottony, too. Angel had hold of the wall in the hallway behind me, and she didn't look any better.

"We have to check for a pulse or something," I said. "Call the ambulance."

"A pulse? Look at her tongue, look at her eyes! I'm not touching her. She's dead!"

"Stop saying that! What if she's having a fit and she just needs to snap out of it? Or in a coma? What if it's like her soap opera person who went into a coma, then boom, she was back, fine."

"Oh, no, she's not going to snap out of this. She's not coming back," Angel said firmly, as though she'd just had a hotline call from the future. "Boom or no boom. She is *dead*."

"She can't be. A mirror. That's how you tell." I backed into the hallway and pulled the shell-framed mirror off its hook. It rattled in my hands.

I took a long breath. Walking those few steps into that room was worse than any nightmare I'd ever had. "Hey,

Louise?" I whispered. "Please wake up." I kept my eyes away from her face, but I saw it anyway, and I knew right then I was going to remember it the rest of my life: her skin beige, as if it were carved from chalk, her tongue swollen, a strand of bleached hair caught in her teeth. Two flies on her bottom lip. It looked like they were wobbling around, but it might have been that tears had filled my eyes.

I locked my gaze on her slippers, hanging off her purple feet, and leaned in with the mirror. The flies lifted. My knee brushed something cool and stiff and I flinched. Her fingers were sticking out, as if reaching for her coffee. I screamed and dropped the mirror and leaped back to the doorway, my heart pounding so hard, my chest actually hurt.

"Okay, she's dead," I said, when I could speak. I turned my head to the kitchen and forced myself to breathe in and out. The air coming through the screen door was so clean, carrying the scent of the pink roses that swayed by the steps as if nothing in the world could be wrong. I filled my lungs with that clean, nothing-could-be-wrong air.

Angel grabbed my arm. "What are you going to do about"—she waved her hand into the den—"about *that*...?"

"She's a person, Angel. That's Louise."

"Fine. What are you going to do about Louise?"

"Why is it *my* job to do something about it? About her."

The instant the question was out of my mouth, though, I knew the answer: I barely knew her, but Louise was my family.

Angel shrugged. "Finders keepers."

"We have to call nine one one."

Angel stared at me. "Be-*cause* . . . ?"

I stared back at her.

"Nine one one's for an emergency, Stella. As in something's going to happen if they don't get here fast. She's dead. She's not going to get any deader."

"We have to call the police. We found a dead person."

"*You* found a dead person." Angel looked like she was thinking hard. "But what if we didn't? What if we hadn't come home till the nighttime? What if we played sports or something? What if we never checked in this room, and she just sat there, croaked—"

"Angel, we have to call the police. It's a law or something!"

Angel turned back to look at Louise again and shuddered. "I know."

My heart sank when she agreed—as if her words had cut the only string it hung from in my chest. I backed into the kitchen and picked up the phone. For a minute, though, I couldn't do anything but look at my hand holding that phone. Someone had called 911 on a cold afternoon two months ago, and the police had come, and the Family Services people had taken me away, and then they tracked down my mother and all that stuff had happened in court. A 911 call had wrecked my whole life.

Angel's hand, slapping over mine on the phone, thumbing the end-call button, brought me back. One look at her face, and I knew she had her own bad memories. "Ten minutes," she said. "Give me ten minutes. Come on. Please," she begged.

I followed her up to her room. She'd snatched her backpack from the hall, and now she dumped it out, strewing books and papers and lunch wrappings everywhere. She bunched a fistful of T-shirts from a drawer and stuffed them into the backpack. Then she crouched to drag some cutoffs from under her bed, then a pair of pink flip-flops.

A sudden memory sprang up. The night of my mother's birthday. I'd followed her up to her bedroom and found her packing in a frenzy, just like this. Her throat wore an inky chain from the necklace I'd made her. She'd tossed it on the bed, the crushed berries staining the white quilt like bruises. It wasn't the first time she'd left, but it was the first time I'd recognized what was happening. The skin on the back of my neck began to prickle. "Don't go!"

My mother swept an armload of clothes from their hangers. When she bent to stuff them into her suitcase, I grabbed the necklace and crammed it under the mattress, my seven-year-old heart pounding. She wouldn't leave without it, I thought. It made her feel enchanted. She didn't even look for it, though. She just zipped the bag.

I remembered feeling the sudden panic of not having the earth beneath me anymore. The sense that my skin was ringing in alarm. I grabbed her wrist. "Don't go!"

She'd shaken me off, then given me a glancing hug on the way out the door. "Go find your grandmother."

"You're just going to leave me?" I'd said the same words then, too.

"Six homes," Angel said, shoving the flip-flops into the backpack without turning around. She sprang back to her bureau and swept in her hairbrush and a couple of elastics, overturned the cigar box she kept her jewelry in. "Six homes. That's enough."

She turned around then. Tears streamed down her cheeks. It looked all wrong, and I realized I'd never seen Angel cry before. But then, she had never seen *me* cry either. Nobody had. I'd stopped doing it after my grandmother had died. After there was no one left to wrap her arms around me when I did it.

I sank to Angel's bed and watched her in the mirror. Angel dropped the backpack after a minute and sank to the other side of the bed. It struck me that if the two girls in the mirror had really just found a dead body, they should look different somehow.

"Where are you going?"

Angel wiped her face with the backs of her hands, then reached under her mattress and pulled out an envelope. "New York. My aunt just got there. She came over from Portugal. For me. She's learning English, and when she gets us a place, Family Services says I can live with her." She drew the letter out of the envelope and smoothed it. "She says, '*É o meu destino agora*.' 'It is my destiny now.'"

She folded the letter and slid it into her backpack. "I'm her destiny, see? I'll just arrive a little early, that's all."

"She's really dead," I said, the words a complete surprise to me.

"She's really dead. And they're really going to take us away." Angel stood and zipped up the backpack.

"Us?"

"Well, they won't let you stay here. They'll dump you with another relative."

"I don't think I have any others."

"A foster home, then. Like me." Angel slung her backpack over one shoulder. "Except not me."

I got up, too, feeling the alarm bells stinging on my neck. *Don't go*. "Do you have money, Angel? It's going to be night. . . ." *Don't go*.

"You could run, too," Angel said. "Someone will find her soon enough."

Run? Where? My mother was somewhere between here and California.

Angel shook her head and left, clattering down the stairs.

I followed her. "It'll be night," I repeated, stupidly.

Angel picked up her jacket from the kitchen chair and tied it around her waist. She looked around the room, and I could tell she was thinking about how it was the last time she'd see it. The expression on her face was hard to read, except that it made me feel sick with loneliness. The alarm bells were shrilling now.

She grabbed the doorknob. "Just don't call for a little while. Ten minutes, okay?"

I looked over at the phone, remembered that other 911 call. How the alarm bells had mixed with police sirens until I couldn't tell them apart.

"Stella! Give me a head start. Okay?" she asked.

I felt the words gathering and knew what they meant, how wrong it was. But I reached out and grabbed her sleeve anyway. "Don't go! I won't call tonight. Tomorrow is Saturday, Angel. Go then."

CHAPTER

◇ 4 ◇

It's hard to sleep with a dead person sprawled out in the room below you. I didn't remember falling asleep at all, but I must have, because how else could I have awakened all those times . . . and remembered, again and again. Each time, I'd lie in the dark praying hard that I would hear a sigh from the den, and then the heavy creak of Louise hauling herself out of her chair and plodding up the stairs to bed.

Angel was stuffing a half-empty package of Fig Newtons into her backpack when I came downstairs the next morning. She looked the way I felt. She shouldered her backpack, then blew some hair away to look back at me.

She started to say something, but I raised my hand. "I remember. I'll wait fifteen minutes and then I'm going to call. Go."

"And you'll tell them I stayed over at a friend's, but you don't know which one. Right?"

"Right. I came home late last night, after something at school—"

"After a rehearsal. For the play. Like we said," Angel insisted.

"I know. I'll remember. And I just found her now. Go, Angel. Get out of here."

There was a knock at the front door. Angel and I both jumped, and she dropped her backpack. We froze, gaping at the door. I was sure it was the police, come to arrest us. My stomach started to heave, as though everything inside me had just been cut loose. The door swung open before either one of us could move.

It was an old guy, dressed in regular work clothes, not a police uniform. He poked his head into the living room. "Louise, you ready?" he called. Then he saw us. He waved into the kitchen. "Morning, girls," he said. "Pretty day."

I risked a glance at the closed den door and gulped back a hysterical giggle—it was so *not* a pretty day.

A dog barked. The old guy leaned back out to yell, "Hold on, Treb." Then he turned back to us. "Is Louise ready?"

Angel walked into the living room. "Who are you?"

"George Nickerson." He stuck out his hand. Angel crossed her arms and glared at him until he dropped it. "I own the cottages next door? Didn't Louise tell you I'd be here this morning?"

"She did," I said. When I have to lie, I get really nervous, and my mouth goes into blabbing mode. "Oh, yeah, she's been talking about it for days. 'Oh, by the way,' she said, 'George Nickerson will be over on Saturday. He owns the cottages next door.'"

Walking closer, I realized he wasn't so old after all. His wrinkles looked like the kind people got from being outside a lot. He had gray hair, but he was like Heloise that way—her silver hair fooled you. "She definitely told us. But she's sick today," I said.

"Sick?" He smiled as if he figured Louise was pulling a fast one on him. "That's convenient . . . the day we open up. Now where is she?"

He took another step in, but Angel moved to block him. "She's lying down. She can't even move. You have to leave."

"We're opening the cottages," he repeated. "I only have the weekend, and there's a lot to do." He walked to the stairs and called up. "Louise?"

"We're going to do it," I said. Angel spun around to shoot me a glare, but I didn't see any other way. Besides, my blabber mode had really kicked in. "That's what she told us: 'You girls help open those cottages, since I'm sick.' She told us to help you open up the cottages today, Mr. Nickerson."

Mr. Nickerson cocked his head to eye me. "You're the niece, right?" he asked.

"Great-niece," I said. "Stella. And this is Angel. We're ready to help open the cottages for my great-aunt. Who's just sick today, that's all." I held my breath and tried to look innocent and helpful.

After a minute, he shrugged and lifted a bunch of keys from his belt and thumbed up a long iron one. "All right, then. This is the master." He pointed over my shoulder to an identical key hanging from a hook beside the door. "That's yours. Grab it. And my name is George, okay?"

"Okay. Got it. George." I wrapped my fingers around the key, hard and knobby as bone, and thought suddenly of Hansel and Gretel, of how they fooled the witch.

We followed George out to his beat-up green truck, parked next door in front of the cottages. He opened the cab door and a yellow lab bounded out and tore around in circles, as if he'd just been sprung from prison. George pulled a wooden sign, painted with the words LINGER LONGER COTTAGE COLONY, from the bed of the pickup and headed over to the signposts next to the road.

The cottages were laid out in a semicircle at the bottom of the horseshoe driveway next to Louise's house. When I'd first arrived, I had tried peering into the windows, but all the shades were down. "Puh! You'll see 'em soon enough," Louise had answered when I'd asked to go inside. "You'll be sick of the sight of them, after you've done a couple of changeovers this summer."

As George hung the sign, I noticed for the first time that the cottages were identical, except for the names lettered above the front doors: SANDPIPER, TERN, PLOVER, and GULL. Identical. The same pink roses climbed up the shingled sides of each one and tumbled down again; all the trim was whitewashed, and the doors all the same pale blue. Everything about the scene looked old and soft, as if it had been drawn in pastel. Lucky Charms colors, I'd called them when I was little.

It looked as if the same artist had drawn George—he wore a faded blue denim shirt rolled up at the sleeves and paint-spattered khaki pants. His hair was a little shaggy, as if he was the kind of person who liked it short, and he kept meaning to get to the barber, but it just hadn't happened for a while. George belonged with these cottages, and so did his dog, with his soft sandy fur, snuffling in the hydrangea bushes beside us.

Angel, on the other hand, looked like a neon sign with her hot-pink tank top and lime-green track pants. Beside her, I probably looked like a pencil sketch with my gray cut-off sweats and my black T-shirt and my boring brown hair. Neither of us fitted in with the Linger Longer cottages, settled there along their good-luck horseshoe driveway. No connections. Anyone could see that.

"Well, what are we waiting for?" George said. "Those cottages aren't going to open themselves, you know."

With each step away from our house, and what was in the den, I felt lighter and calmer. George unlocked the first cottage, Tern, and waved us inside. His dog took off to sniff out the place, but George stayed put in the entryway. "Now, Louise said you two might be helping out with the changeovers this year. We talked Thursday. She didn't say a word about feeling poorly, so it musta come on sudden."

I caught Angel's eye when he said Louise's name, and she looked as guilty as I was feeling.

George didn't seem to notice, though. "We might as well go over things from the beginning," he said. He pointed to a long iron key hanging from a hook on the inside of the door. It looked like the master keys, except for a waxy paper disk, hand-lettered with TERN, tied to it. "They show up, you open the cottage with your master, you hand 'em this key—their key. You remind 'em of what's in the agreement: They lose that key, it's fifty dollars, period. Only one locksmith on Cape Cod I even know of who'll make a key like that anymore. It hasn't happened in at least twenty years—hard to lose a key that big, I guess, but still, that's the rule, okay?"

Angel and I nodded. Then George walked around, snapping up the shades and shoving open the windows. Dust motes whirled up through bars of sunlight against dark wood paneling. I looked around the brightening cottage. Three doors stood open on the back wall: two tiny bedrooms and a bathroom. The room we were standing in had a living area over to the left and kitchen stuff on the right. The kitchen was painted white. It had just room for a table with four chairs, and barely enough counter space to make a sandwich. You'd have to be efficient in a place like this; you could only have the essentials, and you'd have to keep things tidy. I liked that.

"Now, checkout time." George tapped a yellowed notice on the wall. "It's ten o'clock, no exception, because the next tenants come in at three. That doesn't give you much time for the changeovers."

He paused and then nodded at Angel and me as if we'd just said something and he was agreeing with it. "I'm glad she's got you two this year. Tell the truth, I've been a little worried about her, what with her heart."

Angel and I exchanged a quick glance at that.

"Her heart?" I asked. "What's the matter with her heart?"

"Never mind. I shouldn't have said anything. But you two do the heavy cleaning, all right?" George said. "Course, that means you keep the tips—don't go splitting 'em with her if all she's doing is running the laundry through, you doing all the rest."

"Tips?" It was the first time since we'd left the house that Angel had said a word. There was a look in her eyes I couldn't figure out—like she was just now waking up. "They leave tips?"

George nodded with a little chuckle. "Usually. Depends on what hoodlums their kids were. Cleaning fee's built into the rental charge—they already paid it. Louise says they tip outta guilt: Their kids track sand everywhere, fill the teacups with hermit crabs, leave Popsicles melted on the furniture, that kinda thing. Fifteen, twenty dollars—you should ask her, though. I'd better get the linens."

"Each cottage?" Angel asked, and I could practically see her ears perk up. "Each cottage leaves fifteen or twenty dollars? Each week?"

"That's about right. I'll get those linens now." And before we could think of anything to stop him, George left.

Angel and I sprang to the window. I could tell by her

face she was as scared to death as I was. But he didn't go toward our house, only to his truck. "Maybe we should tell him," I said, my heart still hammering in my chest and my legs going cottony again, as if a puff of wind could knock me off my feet. "Angel, I'm scared."

Angel stared at me, looking like she was caught between snarling and fainting. Before she could do either, George was back, talking over a stack of sheets and towels as if he'd never left. "There are two twins and a double in each cottage. Three sets of sheets, three blankets. Towels for four."

He went into the bedroom on the right and we followed. The room was barely big enough for two twin beds and a narrow bureau under the window between them. A row of hooks hung over one bed, and a bookshelf over the other. George dumped the linens on a bed. "There's a backup set of everything, means you don't have to do the wash at changeover time. Store the extras up in the main house, otherwise they get musty—can't help it in the cottages, no heat, so close to the water. That's the next thing. . . ." George nodded out toward the kitchen. "We'll have to give the counters and cabinets in the kitchens and bathrooms a good wash. They're all cleaned in September, but things get a little moldy over the winter—"

"Bleach kills mold!" If I hadn't still been so nervous, I would never have blurted that out with Angel standing there. I bit my lip before I could say anything else, but it was too late—Angel was rolling her eyes, setting up for a sarcastic remark about Heloise.

But George spoke before it came to her. "That's right. That's exactly what we use. It's in the shed. I don't leave it out, all these kids coming," he said. "What'd you say your name was?"

I told him.

"Stella. 'Stella by Starlight.' I'll remember that."

And then I didn't care that Angel was in the room. "You know that song? My father named me after that! He thought it was the prettiest song in the world."

"It is—that's the truth," George said. "Pretty song for a pretty girl." He dropped his head then, as if he was worried he'd said something wrong. I smiled at him to show him he hadn't, and he smiled back—a nice smile, which crinkled his eyes nearly closed. "Your daddy's got good taste," he said.

I fought to keep my smile in place, but my mouth filled with salty water, as if I'd been hit by a wave.

"Oh, now . . . oh, now, sorry," George said. He took a step toward me, and then shoved his hands into his pockets. "Stupid of me. . . . I guess if you're here, he's not . . . I'm sorry."

I swallowed. "It's okay. I never knew him. Bleach and

36

soap," I said. "I'll start in the bathroom." And I walked out, keeping my back straight.

In the bathroom, though, I forgot about everything. I know it sounds crazy to think that a tiny bathroom could fill a person with joy, but this one did. The pine boarding was painted a pale yellow, the color of butter. Whenever I'd pictured the perfect house, it was this exact color. The shelves and windowsills were whitewashed, and the curtains were checkered crisp blue and white. I raised the window and a breeze immediately pillowed the curtains out, as if the room had been waiting all these months to take a nice breath of fresh air.

The bathroom reminded me of a summer day at the beach, with all those sunny colors and the salty breeze. And with all those seashells.

A huge clamshell, cupped like a palm, sat beside the sink ready to hold a bar of soap. Drifts of various shells ran along the windowsill and the long, narrow shelf that spanned the whole wall; they were mounded on top of the medicine cabinet and heaped at the clawed foot of the sink. I wondered how many kids it had taken over how many summers to fill this bathroom.

I picked up a little moon snail shell. It spiraled down, as if it knew where it was going, as if the center of all things was right inside itself. I had a funny urge to swallow it, to make all that perfect wholeness part of me. Instead, I pressed it to my cheek, felt its cool, smooth thinness, and closed my eyes.

Suddenly I was aware of someone in the doorway. I dropped the shell, and it cracked on the tile floor.

George set a jug of bleach down and gathered up the pieces and laid them back on the shelf.

"I broke it," I said. "And it was so beautiful."

"Oh, I like the broken ones fine," George said. He picked up a sand dollar. It was bleached white, at least four inches across, pretty as a sugar cookie. He snapped it in half, and I gasped.

George held the palm of his hand out to me and tapped the broken shell over it. A tiny white chip fell out, and then another. "Look here," he said. "Inside here, these are the teeth. They look like doves, don't you think? A lot of folks take the sand dollar as a message about God and Jesus and all—the nail holes of the cross on the shell, the little doves inside, you see—and that's all right, I guess. But what I see are the doves being released. Now, I see a broken shell and I remind myself that something might have needed setting free. See, broken things always have a story, don't they?"

I shrugged. I didn't think I agreed with him, but I liked imagining it might be true.

"Place like this, families on vacation—well, you'd better

get used to things getting broken. Why, I keep a stack of bed slats in the shed because five or six get broken every year. Kids just have to jump on beds, I suppose."

"You could put a sign up," I said. "No jumping on the beds!"

George laughed hard at that. "Oh, no," he said. "I wouldn't even want to live in a world where kids don't jump on beds. No, I don't mind any of the broken things. I like to figure out their stories." He turned away then, as if he was embarrassed he'd said too much, and set the sand dollar halves carefully back on the shelf.

I didn't think he'd said too much. In fact, if things were different, I thought there might be a lot more I would want to ask him about broken things. Or whatever else he wanted to talk about.

CHAPTER 5

There sure was a lot to do. We laid out cakes of Ivory in their waxy wrappers by the sinks, hung dish towels on wooden spindles, filled salt and pepper shakers, lined cupboards with fresh shelf paper and garbage pails with trash bags, made beds, and checked lightbulbs. We swept down cobwebs and escorted hundreds of daddy long-legs outside, and set mousetraps under the sinks. "Mice," George muttered. "They'd walk away with these cottages, you give them half a chance."

I kept stealing nervous glances at Angel, sure she would just disappear. The funny thing was, she didn't act at all concerned about losing the morning. She trotted along with George, looking fascinated at whatever he was saying and happy to do whatever he asked. I could barely recognize her as the girl who would sulk and glare her way through a silent weekend. And she sure didn't look at all like a girl who was itching to get onto the Mid-Cape Highway heading west. That girl could lie with her whole self.

Finally, George said, "That does it." We went outside and he explained the plan. "There are three cottages left, and three of us. You know what to do now. I'll take Gull; Miss Angel, you take Plover; and Sandpiper is yours, Stella by Starlight. Okay?"

We nodded, but I could see Angel didn't like the plan very much. I tried to catch her eye so I could tell her she should just slip away, but she had turned to follow George, who was opening up Plover for her.

I unlocked Sandpiper's door and headed to the kitchen to get started. The oilskin tablecloth sprigged with strawberries struck me first. Then the cat-shaped cookie jar. I spun around. A stack of puzzles centered on the lobster-pot coffee table in front of the gold plaid couch— yes. In the bedroom: a lighthouse lamp—yes. In the bathroom, two brass anchor hooks, a seahorse shower curtain—yes!

I flew over to Plover, yanked open the screen door, and ran inside.

"Oh my God!" I cried.

"What? What?" I could hear Angel calling behind me, but I was already flying over the lawn to Gull and banging open the door. Inside, I went from room to room, still barely believing it.

George was running water into a pail in the kitchen. He turned when he heard me. "Something wrong?" he asked.

"They're all . . . they're all the same!" I laughed.

"Well, a course they are. It's a cottage colony."

"No, I mean they're *exactly* the same! Exactly!"

George put his pail down to study me. "And you like that, huh?"

"Yes, sir. I like that a lot." Which was an understatement.

George broke into a slow smile. "I could use a break, Stella by Starlight," he said. He sat at the kitchen table and patted the chair beside him. I sat down. He started to pull out his pipe but seemed to have second thoughts about smoking in here and took out a couple of toothpicks instead. He offered me one, and I put it in the corner of my mouth the way he did and tried to act as though I chewed toothpicks all the time.

"All right then," he said when he had worked the

toothpick to where he wanted it. "My parents built this place before I was born. In the forties, right after the war. The soldiers were back, everybody was getting married and having babies. People wanted to go on vacations again, and they sure loved to go places in their big cars. But things were still scarce after the rationing and all. My mother drew up one set of plans, handed them to my father, and said, 'Buy four of everything. It's cheaper that way.'

"The cottages are sixteen feet square—no bigger than your average living room. Lumber came in sixteen-foot lengths then, so no waste. The bedrooms—now the bedrooms are an architectural marvel, as far as I'm concerned. They're six feet by eight feet. But they've got everything you need: a place to sleep, a place to hang your clothes, a shelf for books, a light to read by. And the bathrooms are only four feet wide. I tell you, my mother was a genius. She insisted everything be plain; you can see that. She knew people wouldn't mind that in a vacation place. Look at this." George pointed to a cabinet behind him.

I nodded.

"That's knotty pine for you. It's cheap, 'cause the knotholes bleed sap through forever. Probably ten coats of paint on these cabinets. And it still bleeds through." He leaned back and gazed around the cottage. "I keep wondering if I should update, put in televisions or internet, modernize.

But everybody who stays here says no, don't change a thing, it's so peaceful. So there you are. Plain and simple, and all exactly the same, since 1946."

"And then you were born?" I prompted. I wasn't ready to stop listening to him.

George shifted the toothpick to the other side of his mouth, nodding. "Yep. I was one of those babies everybody was having after the war. Boomers. I'm sixty-four—probably too old to be fishing for a living, but too late to learn anything else, I guess."

I rolled my toothpick to my other cheek. "Sixty-four's not too late to learn things," I said. "How old was Louise?"

I felt my face drain. "I mean how old *is* she? I mean, *was* she when you met her."

George didn't notice. "Oh. She's been managing the cottages for . . . oh, maybe twenty-five years. More. I don't even know. Since my folks died. But I guess you'd better ask *her* that question. . . . I'm not telling a woman's age on her. I may be old, but I'm not a fool."

George got up then, and I followed him to the door. And then I realized something important. "My mother stayed here for two years, about twenty years ago. She was about eight or nine. Do you remember her?"

"Twenty years is a long time ago," George said, leaning against the door frame and squinting into the sun. "I was

44

lobstering then—gone a lot. Sorry."

He really did look sorry about that, so I smiled at him again. "That's okay. Well, back to work." I started across the lawn.

George called out. "Wait, now. Kind of a hellion, always in trouble? But she had a soft heart, always carting around some baby animal she'd rescued. Your mother?"

I turned back. "You remember her?"

"Not much, really. But I do remember complaining to Louise one summer. This kid was supposed to be helping, but she went around with a twig springing every mouse-trap I set. I finally gave up." He laughed at the memory, then cocked his head and eyed me. "Your mother. Yeah. Now I see it."

I walked back to Sandpiper glowing with the things I could tell my mother when she called. "George remembers you. We opened the cottages—you did that, too. Remember the mousetraps?"

I stood on the step of Sandpiper—my cottage—and squared my shoulders and took a deep breath. And then I got to work. I prepared that little house with affection and all my skill, as if the president of the United States himself was going to pull in here a week from now. When I was finished, I looked around at what I had done and my heart just about burst from pride. The cottage seemed to smile back at me, as if it was proud, too. I walked around, putting on the final touches: I pushed the kitchen curtains open a little more to give a better view, shifted the kitchen chairs out so they'd seem more welcoming to tired travelers, and turned down the beds. Then I locked the door and left.

In Plover, I found Angel sitting on one of the twin beds, tangled in sheets.

"I can't. . . . It's all . . . uuggghhh!" she groaned.

I picked up the knot of sheets. "Do you want to go? George is setting up the grills. He won't know. I could still say you had to visit a friend, and I just found her. . . ."

"No." Angel stood up and found a pillowcase and stuffed a pillow into it. Sideways. "Just help me."

We were hosing off the picnic tables when George came over. He took out a pocketknife and scraped at some hard green stuff on the boards. "Frass." The way he said it, it sounded like a swear. "Darned gypsy moths, droppings everywhere." Then he looked at his watch.

"Almost three," he said. "I gotta be at the boatyard. We're done for the day anyway. You did a good job, girls. Go get yourselves some lunch and have Louise give me a call tonight." Then he whistled for Treb, who was napping in Plover's shade, and climbed into his truck. We walked back to the house but didn't go in. We sank to the brick steps together and watched his pickup grow smaller, until it disappeared.

"I feel bad for him," I said. "Pretty soon, he'll find out. First he'll be sad, because I think they're sort of friends. And then it'll hit him that he's got nobody to run this place." I braced myself, realizing I had just committed the giant sin of talking to Angel.

But Angel just leaned over her knees and picked a chip of mortar off the step. She slid a glance at me through her hair. "Or not."

"Of course he'll find out. The police will call him first thing."

"No, I mean . . ." Angel tucked her hair behind her ear to look at me hard, as if she was trying to decide something. "What if we did it? Took care of things here for a while?"

"What are you talking about?"

"You heard him. Fifteen or twenty dollars each cottage, each week. I need money. I need three hundred fifty dollars for . . . well, I just need it. I could earn it here. And I wouldn't have to go to another dumb foster home while my aunt's getting a place. . . ."

I couldn't say the obvious, but I didn't have to.

"I know," said Angel. "We couldn't do it. I was just wishing." She flicked the mortar chip into the roses and wrapped her arms around her knees.

I looked over at the horseshoe of cottages, thinking about how welcoming we'd left them, how happy the families arriving next Saturday were going to be. And suddenly I found myself wishing we could stay, too. Not for the money, but because I wanted to see those families pile in. And because I wanted to spend a little more time where my mother had been.

But then I remembered what was in the den. "No," I said, "we couldn't do it."

"Never," Angel agreed. "Stupid idea."

We sat there for a minute, looking down the empty road. Angel was probably thinking, In a few minutes I'm on my way. I was thinking that I kind of liked this new Angel, the girl who talked to me. And that in a few minutes I would be left alone. With . . .

"Because it would be too hard," Angel said.

"Impossible."

"I mean, I didn't even *understand* half of what he was saying, never mind be able to do it."

I turned to Angel. "Who? Do what?"

Angel stared at me. "George! Run the cottages. Do all that changeover stuff he was talking about?"

It was my turn to stare. "No, Angel, that part would be easy. It's . . ." I waved my hands behind me.

"Louise? Oh, Louise just needs to be buried. We had

to bury a goat once. It wasn't even ours—it just wandered into our yard and died. Are you serious about us being able to do it, run things?"

"She's not a goat, Angel! She's my great-aunt!"

"I know that. I'm just saying, you dig a big hole . . ."

I jumped up and brushed the brick grit from the backs of my thighs. "You're crazy. It's time. I'm going to call the police, so you'd better get going."

Angel got up, too. "Right, okay. I'll get my stuff."

Angel went in, but I didn't follow her. I didn't like watching people leave.

I fingered the master key in my pocket, and then I walked back over to the cottages. One by one, I opened them up. In each, I took a knife from the silverware drawer, crawled under the kitchen and the bathroom sinks, and sprang the mousetraps.

And then I closed up all the cottages, each lock snapping shut with a satisfying double clink: "There, *yes*." "There, *yes*." As I walked down the driveway, I noticed what a nice sound that was, too: the bleached white shells crunching under my sandals. I stopped. I had been here only eight weeks, but I suddenly knew that I would miss this place. Louise's house, a little worn-down maybe, but always clean and orderly, like my grandmother's had been. The four Lucky Charms cottages, nestled under the oaks and pines. Through the trees, in the distance, the Mill River winding like a silver ribbon through the marsh that had turned so green in the past month, it could hurt your eyes. Beyond that, the ocean, dark blue as rinsed jeans today. The air was salty and sweet—seaweed and honeysuckle. How had I never noticed all this before? I locked it all into place so I could visit it whenever I needed to, like my icebergs.

I let myself in the kitchen door, but before I picked up the phone to call the police, I sat down at the table with a sheet of paper, a ruler, and a pencil. Another few minutes wouldn't matter, I figured. I drew an eight-inch square. At a half inch to a foot, I copied the floor plan of those cottages: the two-inch-wide bathroom lying snugly against the three-inch-wide bedrooms, the kitchen area on the right, the living room on the left.

Everything fitted.

I brought the drawing up to my room and tucked it into my Hints folder. As I was about to go back downstairs to make the call, I heard a crash from Louise's bedroom. The door was open. Angel was pulling things down from the closet shelf.

"I thought you were gone."

"Almost. I'm looking for something." She tossed out a stuffed garbage bag.

I stepped into the room. I'd never been inside before, only stood in the doorway a few times, talking to Louise. It was dark—the curtains were drawn—and too flowery: flowered drapes, flowered bedspread, flowered robe on the hook. The flowers looked wilted somehow—as if without Louise to tend them, they were dying.

Another garbage bag went sailing out. "Two bags of old panty hose," Angel's voice followed. "Gross."

I ran my fingers over the photographs lined up on the bureau. Louise at different ages, posing with different people. One in a worn silver frame showed her at about ten, with her arms around a little girl in red shorts sitting beside her. The little girl was holding a book on her lap, a finger slipped inside to hold a page. I picked up the photo. It was my grandmother, I knew.

"There must be fifty pairs of shoes in here," Angel said. "And all she ever wore were those sneakers with the toes out! There are a hundred dresses, and what did she wear every day? That ratty bathrobe!"

I rubbed my thumb over the tarnished frame. All it needed was a little toothpaste to bring the shine back—I suddenly could see that hint in my folder. The folder I'd inherited from my grandmother. My grandmother who was the little girl with Louise in the photo in the tarnished silver frame. Another triple tie. I sank to the bed, anchored with the good weight of it.

Angel came back with her arms full and sat down beside me. "Who has eighteen pocketbooks?" she said. "With, like, twelve cents in each?"

I stared at the photo and wondered what book my grandmother had been reading that day.

"It's not stealing, you know. She's been paid all this money to feed me and stuff." Angel dumped out a purse beside me. "Well, I guess most of it is *yours*, actually."

"Were there any photo albums in the closet, Angel?" I asked.

Angel pushed a big straw bag over to me. "I mean, it's your inheritance, right? You and your mother are going to get all her stuff. And the house, right? Um . . . Stella?"

"What?" I said, tearing my gaze from my grandmother's little-girl face.

"This house. If you don't have any other relatives, then neither does she. You and your mother are going to inherit it."

The meaning of her words took shape in slow motion.

We were going to inherit this house.

Move into it and live here.

Not have to leave it.

Everything clicked into place like abacus beads. Until the final bead: my mother.

And then my movie rolled out. I'd been making it up for the past two years.

In it, my mother walks into our kitchen. I don't recognize the kitchen, but I know it's ours. It's bright in there, and clean, and everything is neat and in its place. It smells really good—even in my movie you can tell somehow—because I'm cooking something nice. My mother walks in, and she smiles. She takes off her jacket and hangs it over a chair, and she leans over to see what's in the pot I'm cooking. In my movie, my mother looks so peaceful to be there. She's not pacing around, she's not darting looks out the window like she's getting that itch to be somewhere else. She sighs, she's so peaceful. And then she looks over at me as if she can't believe how lucky she is. As if she's just won the Mega-Jackpot in the lottery of daughters. "Hey, Stella," she says, in an amazed voice. An amazed but *peaceful* voice. A not-going-anywhere voice. "Hey, Stella, we're home."

And then my mother looks at me harder. She sees that I am almost twelve. I can take care of myself, and her, too, now. She can tell I could make us a home now, easy.

I'd never known the kitchen in my movie, but now I did—Louise's, right downstairs. Ours. I'd never known the opening scene of my movie, how we got this house, but now I did—I was meant to keep our home for my mother, to prove to her that I could, until she came back.

We were meant to live here.

I stood, my legs shaking a little. Not from fear this time, but from all the hope that had suddenly welled up. I lifted the pocketbook from Angel's lap and tossed it onto the sea of lipstick tubes, candy wrappers, and crumpled tissues.

"Angel," I said. "Let's do it."

CHAPTER

6

"For real?"

"For real."

"How come?"

I took a deep breath, thinking. "Because you're right. My mother's going to inherit this place. And that's great—except she's not here."

"So call her."

"I can't. She's . . . traveling." And of course she never could keep a cell phone. The truth was, I didn't know where she was. She'd called last Saturday, halfway to California. A job working with horses, she said. Actually, she'd said a

55

possible job. That "possible" had worried me.

"Well, so what? They're not going to give it to some-body else."

I walked over to the corner window and pushed the curtains open. I rested my fingertips and my forehead on the panes. The last time I hadn't felt the world was made of glass and it was my job to keep it from shattering had been when we'd lived in a house a lot like this. My mother had let that house go, but somehow it felt like it was my fault. Now I needed a home to prove that I wouldn't make the same mistakes again, whatever they were. I couldn't tell Angel any of this, though.

I looked over the cottages. Here were *five* homes to prove myself on. Below, in our backyard, were Louise's blueberry bushes. My mother's blueberry bushes. Mine, too, now. I felt a good iron-bone, lead-blood heaviness settle me into the floorboards. I couldn't tell Angel any of this, either.

I turned. "Because, this place?" I said instead. "I'm not leaving it."

The first thing, of course, was Louise.

We opened the door of the den cautiously. Angel threw her arms across her face and staggered back. "She stinks."

"I know," I said.

"No, I mean she really *stinks*."

"I know, Angel. She's dead. She can't help it."

"Well, does Heloise have any good hints about that?"

I was all ready to give Angel the fight she was looking for, but then I realized she was actually on the right track. "Be right back," I told her. In the laundry I found what I needed. "Febreze," I explained, spraying a good blast into the den. A cloud of flies buzzed up from Louise's corpse in irritation. "Eliminates odors for a freshness that fills your home."

"Well, we're still going to have to bury her now. Where do you think?"

"In her garden," I said right away. "She'd like to be out there, I think. And there's an empty row in the back she was saving for the late lettuces. But—"

"Let's get digging, then."

"No. We have to . . . get her ready or something."

"You're right. When my dog Max died, we put on his rhinestone collar."

"She's not a dog, Angel. She's not a dog and she's not a goat."

"I know. But I bet she'd want to be dressed up. I bet she wouldn't want to spend forever in that ratty robe."

Angel left the room and came back with her palms dripping with sparkling jewelry. "The Home Shopping

Channel is really going to miss your great-aunt."

I lifted the pieces, trying to remember anything that seemed special. "I never saw her wear any of this. I don't know which she'd choose."

"Choose? We'll put it all on. This is a special occasion."

When it came to doing it, though, we couldn't. Neither one of us could touch Louise's neck or ears or wrists. In the end, we just tossed everything over her robe and then jumped back to the doorway. Her lap looked like a pirate's treasure chest, with necklaces and bracelets spilling all over her, and I thought, who wouldn't like that?

"Okay then," Angel said. "Let's get digging."

"Wait," I said. "You can't just dump a person in the ground. . . ."

"Why not? I bet there are dozens of people buried right in that backyard."

"What are you talking about?"

"Fifth-grade history. The Wampanoag Indians were here on Cape Cod hundreds of years before any Pilgrims ever landed. You think the Wampanoags or the Pilgrims called up the undertaker and said, 'Come and get him!' whenever one of them died? Nope, straight in the ground."

"She's Louise, Angel! She's not a dog and she's not a goat and she's not a Pilgrim and she's not a Wampanoag." I folded my arms across my chest and narrowed my eyes, to show her I meant business.

Angel shook her head like I was the sorriest person she'd ever met. Then she made a big show of huffing off into the kitchen and pulling out the phone book. I followed her because I wanted to know who she was calling. Also, because the Febreze was wearing off.

"Yes, hello . . . Bradford Funeral Home? I'd like some information," Angel said in a voice I'd never heard her use before. It was the voice of someone who actually could be named Angel. "It's for a history report. I'm researching how bodies were prepared for burial on Cape Cod in the olden times. Before undertakers." She shot me a look. "*Not* Wampanoag Indians and not the Pilgrims, though. Other people." Then she listened and said, "I see," and "Fascinating!" a couple of times. Finally she said, "Okay, thanks. I bet I'm going to get an A on my report!" and flipped off the phone.

"Well . . . ?" I asked.

"We have to bury her deep," Angel said firmly.

"All that? That was their advice?"

"No that's *my* advice. We had to bury that goat twice. The first time, it wasn't deep enough and the neighborhood dogs got to it. What a mess, parts all over—"

"Angel! What did they say?"

"Who? The funeral home? Nothing. They weren't

there—it was just a message machine. Now let's go bury her!"

"Not everything's a big joke, Angel! And we can't just go digging a grave at"—I glanced at the kitchen clock—"four in the afternoon. Someone would notice."

"Like who?" Angel cried, exasperated. "We're at the end of a dirt road. No one goes by. Ever."

"Just slow down, Angel!" The thing was, I liked plenty of time to think things through, to imagine everything that could go wrong, before I did something I couldn't undo. "Tonight," I said. "When it gets dark. We'll dig the grave tonight."

"It's not dark until really late—it's like the longest day of the year or something." She looked at the calendar. "Perfect!" she cried. "It actually is the longest day of the year! Louise had great timing. But I'm not hanging around with a corpse until it gets dark. Let's get digging now."

"No. Tonight! Remember, she's *my* relative." So lame. So, so lame.

Angel picked up the phone and thrust it at me. "Call. Call the police now. I'm out of here."

"No! No, wait. You promised." I felt the old Alice-tumbling-down-the-rabbit-hole panic rise. *Don't go.* "You need money, remember?"

"I'll find another way to get it. I'm not going to be

ordered around all summer and have to follow all your stupid rules."

"What rules? I do not have rules!"

"Are you *serious*?" Angel cried. "Do you ever listen to
yourself? 'Never put daffodils in a vase with other flowers—they'll kill them.' 'Never swim in an outgoing tide.'
Actually, you must have a hundred rules about swimming.
'Always store a marshmallow in with the brown sugar so it
won't harden up.' Want me to go on?"

"Those aren't rules, they're hints. Helpful hints."

"Oh, and 'No burying bodies at four in the afternoon!'
is just a helpful hint?" She swung her backpack off the
chair and shouldered it.

"Okay, okay! You're right. From now on, we decide
everything together. Okay?"

There was silence then. For a long time. Angel's fingers
clenched and unclenched around the backpack straps.

"How about this," I tried. "We dig now. If anyone sees
us, I guess it will just look like we're working in the garden.
But we don't . . . you know . . . until it's dark."

"Fine," Angel growled after a minute. She stomped over
to the door and I followed. Both of us just stood silenced
then, looking out. While we had been arguing, it had begun
to rain. The weather was on my side. I bit my cheek so my
relief wouldn't show, but Angel scowled at me anyway.

"Fine," she growled again. "We'll do it tomorrow." She stomped upstairs and stomped back down, pajamas and earphones trailing out of her backpack. She lifted the master key off the hook at the front door. "But I am not spending another night with a dead body."

I dashed through the rain after her, over the yard and into Plover. When she marched into the bedroom with the twin beds, I thought, Good, we can talk a little and I can apologize. She was right—sometimes I did get kind of bossy. Before I could follow her into the room, though, she slammed the door.

Well, fine. Wherever that girl was, I wasn't.

The smell inside was a little musty, even with the lingering bleachy scent of our cleaning, so I raised the windows a little. Not enough to let the rain in, but enough to smell the fresh wet pines outside. As I knelt on the couch, I noticed something: Most of the pillows had tears, raggedly sewn back up. I remembered what George had said about kids on vacation, and wondered how many pillow fights they'd been through. I got up and wandered around then, and everywhere, I saw what he'd been talking about. It was kind of fun to make up the stories behind what was broken. The cookie jar was missing an ear—a hit-and-run cookie thief. The spaghetti pot lid was dented—probably used in battle with the chipped ladle. Two blades of the fan were fresh new wood—I couldn't even imagine what had happened to the old ones.

I went into the open bedroom and lifted the mattress. The slats were half-inch-thick boards—you'd have to jump pretty hard to crack one of those. The thought made me smile. I got into the clean blue sheets we'd put on this morning and thought, I like it in here.

CHAPTER
7

"*Jesus querido!*" Angel dropped the shovel.

I clutched at my heart.

"Sorry, didn't mean to startle you. Back to mow and finish up what we didn't get to yesterday." George climbed over the wire fencing and picked the shovel up, handed it back. He bent the fencing down a little and Treb sailed over it, then dropped to give himself a dirt back rub. He scrambled to his feet and gave us a big dog smile, as if to say, Wasn't I entertaining? Angel and I were still having heart attacks, though, and we ignored him. Treb flopped down and sighed as if he was exhausted from trying to get our attention.

"Now, what she got you planting? A rowboat?" George laughed at his own joke, but we sure didn't. "Something big, anyway."

I looked down at the ground. The three of us standing there threw three early-afternoon shadows that arrowed directly toward the house, as if sending a blaring sign to George. He didn't notice, though. I looked out over the marsh, ordering myself to breathe in, breathe out.

"Pumpkins," Angel said firmly, and started digging again. "We're planting a row of pumpkins. The really big kind. Giant."

That girl. It was terrible to lie, of course. But Angel was so good at it, I couldn't help admiring her.

"Kinda late for pumpkins," George said thoughtfully. "Shoulda gone in Memorial Day. Still, I guess if the frost holds off this fall . . ." He poked around at the beans, their bright-green tendrils curling around the section of lattice Louise had leaned up there. "Louise has a green thumb, I'll give her that. Tomatoes look good."

"Well, we have to get back to work," Angel said. She stabbed the earth, dumping a shovelful right next to George's work boot.

George wasn't too good at taking a hint, though. And he wasn't in any hurry to leave. He leaned back against a fence post, then dug around in his pocket for a pipe and some tobacco. I turned my face away, suddenly certain that *Your friend Louise is dead in the den!* might as well have been written on my forehead. I heard the tiny pop of the match catching, heard the wet rattle of the pipe stem as he drew in to light it. I smelled the tobacco. Breathe in, breathe out. We were just two girls planting pumpkins.

"Pumpkins go in mounds, not rows," he said. "She should know that."

"Yep, she said that," Angel said. "I just forgot."

"Pumpkins have big appetites. You got fertilizer?"

I shot Angel a look, but it was no good, of course. Not with that girl.

"Oh, yeah," Angel said. "We've got a *lot* of fertilizer."

"Good. Well then, you want a thick layer of mulch to keep the weeds down. Seaweed's the best. You tell her she can use my truck if she wants to go down to the beach and pick up a load right now. I'm going to be here awhile, mow the lawn and wash the decks. Never mind, I'll tell her myself. You girls—"

"No!" Angel and I yelled at the same time.

George looked between us, eyes narrowed. "She still sick?"

"Yes," I said at the same time as Angel's "No!"

"I mean, yes," Angel said. "She's still sick, but now she broke her foot."

I whipped around to stare at her.

"Yeah, she was so sick, she lost her balance and fell off the back steps. Actually, I think she might have been . . . you know . . ." Angel tipped back her head and cocked her thumb to her lips, pretending to glug from a bottle.

I had to turn away then. George looked as stunned as I was.

"What a night," Angel went on. "She had to go to the emergency room, got a cast and crutches and everything."

"Drinking, Louise . . ." George shook his head as if the picture wouldn't come into focus. He took a thoughtful pull on his pipe. "Well, that's a lotta woman to have to haul around on crutches. I'd better go see what I can do—"

Angel actually sprang in front of him, blocking his way. "No," she said. "She's asleep. She was up all night—you know, in the emergency room. She'll be mad if anyone wakes her . . . mad at us!"

George turned back to the house. "Something's fishy here, girls," he muttered. "I'll go talk to her." He clamped down on his pipe and started over to the house.

"Hey, that's a great idea about the seaweed," I said. "Let's go now and get some."

I climbed over the fence and headed for George's pickup next door before he could answer. Angel was right behind me. We got into his truck, and I tapped the horn and waved.

George turned on Louise's kitchen step, his hand raised to knock, looking torn. There wasn't much he could do, though, with two girls parked in his truck like eager puppies, ready to go for a ride. He shook his head and came back across the yard. The driver's door opened with a creaky sigh, and Treb jumped onto the bench and wriggled himself in between Angel and me. Then George heaved himself in with his own creaky sigh and cranked up the engine.

"How long she going to be laid up?" he asked, squinting up at the house as we backed past it. "Couldn't be worse timing. I got a boat to run, codfish to chase, a crew to pay. They depend on me—Johnny Baker's wife just delivered twins—and it's a short season. Boat's been hauled out a week, so we're already behind. I miss a single day in summer—a single day—and we all suffer come February, let me tell you. She can't be calling me every ten minutes to come replace a screen, pick up charcoal, that kinda thing."

"Don't worry," Angel said. "She won't be calling you."

I kicked Angel's ankle, and she kicked me back. "As long as she can't walk, we'll take care of things for her," she assured George. She started messing around in the glove compartment, as if that was the end of that discussion. Suddenly she yelped and pulled her hand out with a wounded look.

George reached over and closed the glove compartment. "Sorry. I throw my hooks in there. You all right?" he asked.

"Oh, sure," Angel said, sucking the tip of her finger. "Fine."

"You and Treb." George chuckled. "That's how he got his name, you know. Came up to me on the beach one day, just a puppy, a stray if I ever saw one."

"This dog?" I threw my arm around Treb. "This dog was a stray?"

"This is a *great* dog," Angel said—the first time we had agreed about anything.

Treb lifted his head as though he knew we were admiring him. Angel scratched his ruff. "Who wouldn't want him?"

"Happens all the time on Cape Cod," George said. "People get a puppy while they're on vacation, seems like a good idea. Then by the time they leave for home, they realize they don't want the responsibility. So they just leave it behind when they pack up. Terrible. The way I see it, whoever let this dog go didn't deserve him.

"Anyway, I was bluefishing, and he came up and sat down behind me, waiting for me to turn around. I finally did, and that's when I saw: He had a big treble hook lure hanging from his lip. All three hooks, clean through. Don't know how he managed that. But he sat still and let me snip off the barbs and then pull them through—musta hurt something awful—and he never flinched. This dog hasn't left my side since."

The truck bounced, its engine a gentle growl. It was good riding up high—it made me feel like a little kid somehow. I grew excited: Maybe I'd ridden like this with my father, up high in a truck. I didn't remember it, but that didn't mean it hadn't happened. I was only two when he left. Memories could be locked down deep with little kids. Sometimes you had to dig them out.

Maybe my father had driven me around in a rumbling truck like this back in New Orleans, trombone behind the seat, radio on, singing along with it to his little girl. Maybe he'd pulled over to a club he used to play in, brought me in on his shoulders, introduced me around. I would have been shy, but he would have said, "This is my little girl, my little Stella by Starlight. She sweet or what?"

"Hey." Angel's elbow jab interrupted my thoughts. "You just going to sit in here?"

We were there, at the far end of the Mill River Beach parking lot. George was already dragging the barrels out of the truck bed. I slid out and joined him.

He pulled a rake out. "Only got the one. You girls take a walk. I'll just be a few minutes here." He snapped a leash onto Treb's collar and handed it to me. "Watch him, now. He finds a dead fish, a dead gull, out here, he's gonna roll in it. Once he found a seal. Oh, boy, what a smell—took me a week to wash it out."

I took off toward the water and was surprised when Angel followed. She never went anywhere near the water—didn't even want to look at the ocean from a distance, which was kind of hard to avoid if you lived on Cape Cod. Angel managed: She kept her bedroom shades down, ate her meals at the chair facing the refrigerator, and generally pretended we were living in Kansas.

Angel parked herself on a flat boulder at the base of the first jetty, shoulders hunched as if it were cold, facing away from the sea with her long black hair hanging like drawn drapes. I walked along the edge of the water, Treb trotting beside me, stopping every few feet to nose up some seaweed or sniff at a crab. But then I turned around, feeling guilty. Here I might have just had a memory of my father, while Angel couldn't even look at the ocean.

Angel never once mentioned her father. Louise had told me how he'd died, though: When Angel was seven, he'd gone down with his scalloper in a freak squall. The boat took on water, went down fast. They had an extra hand on board that day, someone's cousin. One more than the boat was fitted out for. As the captain, Angel's father had handed out the survival suits, and because of the extra guy, there hadn't been one for him. He drowned fifteen minutes before the coast guard got there.

"Puh. Cutting corners" was Louise's take. "And with that motherless little girl needing him." She'd scowled into the dishwater as though *she* would have had extra lifesaving gear on board any boat of *hers*.

I walked back and sat down beside Angel. She ignored me as if I were another rock on the jetty, but Treb worked his way between us and sat panting and wet with a satisfied dog smile. I practiced in my head what I might say about her father, about how heroic I thought he was. Before I could find the right words, though, Angel got up and walked away, down the beach. I stroked Treb's ear and watched her.

Angel walked the shoreline, not looking at the water, but not looking inland, either. She was focused on something ahead of her. She drew up behind a huge flock of gulls—maybe a hundred of them—resting on the line of seaweed left by the tide. The gulls were all facing offshore, into the breeze, away from us. They shifted, as if they were a little uneasy with a human so close behind them, then settled down again.

Very deliberately, as though she were a conductor opening a symphony, Angel raised her arms. And all those gulls, all of them, at the very same instant, took flight! Those birds—they were Angel's orchestra. Even from where I sat, a hundred yards behind, I could feel the powerful beating of their wings lifting my heart in my chest like hope.

And through it, Angel just stood there, arms still swept up to the flock wheeling above her. I wished I could see her face.

CHAPTER

8

George dropped us off and went to start the lawn. The first thing I did was waft a fresh coating of Febreze over Louise, spraying extra long, since I didn't think the manufacturers were considering decomposing bodies when they came up with the instructions. I pulled the door shut, hard.

Angel was in the kitchen, staring into the open refrigerator. She took a sleeve of American cheese out and peeled off a couple of slices, then passed it to me. "We missed breakfast. And lunch."

I ate a piece, peering into the fridge next to Angel, and

started calculating. "She shopped on Wednesdays. She cut her coupons in the morning, then headed out before the specials ran out. That means we should have three more days of food."

"More," Angel figured. "Since she's not going to be eating her share."

"It's still not much. There's not much here. Oh, wait. Her hurricane cupboard."

Angel gave me a blank look.

"She used to say that anyone who lived on Cape Cod and didn't stock up in case of a hurricane was a fool. Sometimes she went down there when she needed a can of something. It's in the cellar, that's all I know."

I found it: Next to the laundry, a cupboard with two shelves full of stuff: a tiny canned ham, a giant jar of peanut butter, crackers, maybe half a dozen cans each of tuna fish, beans, and tomatoes, and a five-pound tub of Crisco. There were candles and matches and batteries, too.

I ran back up, bringing the peanut butter. You can eat peanut butter for three meals a day. "We're not going to starve for a while," I said. "Plus, there's her garden."

Angel made a gagging face—she never ate anything green.

"Scurvy is a real thing, you know. It's not just sailors who get it."

Angel rolled her shoulders. She pulled one of her never-ending supply of Dum Dums from her shorts pocket and stuck it in her mouth. She opened the freezer and poked at a red-and-white box.

"Not the coffee cake," I said. "She keeps it there in case."

"In case what? In case she dies and we're hungry?"

"No, in case someone stops by unexpectedly. Didn't you ever listen to her?"

"I tried not to," Angel said. "Blah, blah, blah." She pulled the coffee cake out.

"No," I said, surprised at how strongly I felt. "We are not touching that. It was important to her. She liked to feel prepared."

"She's dead," Angel said, and ripped open the end of the box. "She probably wasn't too prepared about that."

I reached for the box, but Angel yanked it back.

"Don't do it, Angel. I mean it."

Angel eyed me then, trying to decide how far to fight. I set my jaw and folded my arms to let her know.

Angel looked down at the box. "The expiration date is January, anyway," she said. "*Four years ago* January. She didn't get many unexpected visitors, I guess." She tossed the box into the trash.

I picked it out and put it back into the freezer, my lips

pressed tight. Then I went back to studying the refrigerator. "There's a pound of hamburger in here. She always made chili on Sunday afternoons. I guess we should make chili."

Angel snorted a laugh around the Dum Dum.

"What's so funny?"

"You're going to just *make chili*," Angel said. "The kind you could actually eat."

"Of course," I said. "And you're going to help."

I was wrong about that part. I handed Angel a couple of onions and told her to cut them up, and when she handed the cutting board back, the onions were in halves. With the skins on.

"You've never cooked before, Angel?"

Angel's chin shot up and her eyes narrowed.

"Never mind. You can watch."

Angel picked a *Soap Opera Digest* out of the mail basket, hopped onto the counter, and began to read. But I noticed she kept stealing suspicious glances at my hands, as if I were dealing cards and she wanted to catch me cheating. I chopped onions and peppers and slid them into a big cast-iron frying pan with some oil. As I worked, I gave out helpful cooking tips I'd learned from my grandmother, but I made it sound as if I was just talking to myself. "If you keep onions in the refrigerator, they won't make you cry."

Angel kept her head buried in the magazine, but I thought she nodded a little at that.

"Not too much garlic," I went on, mincing a couple of cloves and adding them to the pan. "It can take over. Rubbing your fingers on stainless steel will get the garlic smell out—weird, I know, but it works. I read it in . . . never mind. Brown the hamburger after that." Then I stirred in the tomatoes and beans. "Two big cans each," I said, in case Angel didn't see it. "That's it."

Angel slid off the counter and took two spoons from the silverware drawer.

"No, it has to cook now," I explained. "For a couple of hours."

Angel looked as if she was trying to figure out if I was kidding. Before I could explain the importance of simmering, there was a knock at the screen door. We jumped.

George again. We hadn't noticed the mower kick off. He was holding a shovel. "You're all set," he said, setting it by the steps. "You two helped me out so much yesterday, I figured the least I could do was come back and dig those holes for you."

Treb trotted up the steps then. He began to whine and nose the door. George shook his finger at him. "You're not going in, boy. That's the price you pay for rolling in seaweed. By the way, I piled it beside those holes for you girls.

Just fork it over the mounds when you're done working in your fertilizer."

Treb scratched harder at the door. I shot a quick glance down the hall and shuddered. George ordered him down, and Treb obeyed, but you could tell it nearly killed him. He stared through the screen with his head cocked as if he couldn't believe what he was smelling. Now and then he broke his gaze to look up at George as if to say, Don't you want to *roll* in that? He gave a final scrabble at the door and then lay down with his head on his paws and looked up at us, whimpering at the injustice.

Angel came up behind me. "Well, thanks, George," she said brightly. "Good-bye!"

But George didn't take the hint. He brushed the grass clippings off his pants and then opened the screen door with a *"Stay!"* warning to Treb and stepped inside. He lowered his head and pointed a finger at me. "You," he said.

"Me?"

"Eight mousetraps, all sprung. Not a mouse in a one of 'em. You know anything about that?"

I raised my hands in surrender, relieved. Angel stared between George and me.

"I figured," George said with a smile. "Soft heart for the underdog, runs in the family. Okay, I give up—your underdogs can have the cottages this year." He sniffed.

"Smells good." He crossed to the stove and nodded over the bubbling pot. "Louise makes some fine chili. She must be feeling better if she got up and cooked."

Angel and I stared at each other.

"Gotta be tough on crutches. Guess it wiped her out. Must be why I couldn't raise her."

Now we stared at George.

"I saw her through the window as I was coming in. I waved, but then I could see she was conked out. Dead to the world."

Angel found her voice first. It was shaky, though. "She is. Dead to the world. Exactly. So . . ." She gave a meaningful look at the door.

"I brought my screwdriver," George said, completely ignoring Angel's meaningful look. "I've been promising to fix that towel rack in the bathroom for weeks. Once the boat goes back in tomorrow, I won't have the time, so I'll just do it while I'm here. I'll be quiet—"

My voice came back then. Loud. "No!"

It was George's turn to stare.

"Stella is just remembering the big school project we have to do," Angel said. "It's due tomorrow. Stella can't work if there's someone in the house." If lying were a sport, this girl would have a neckful of gold medals. Angel grabbed the door again and swept her hand as if George were already walking through. "So, bye, thanks."

George finally gave up. "Well, then," he said. "You're all set for Saturday. You have Louise call me if she needs anything."

"Thanks again!" Angel said, shutting the door on him.

We went over to the window and watched him get into his truck with Treb and drive off. "That guy is trouble," Angel said.

"He's really nice."

"Oh, he's nice, all right," Angel agreed. "But he's *in love* with her."

"With who? Louise?"

Angel nodded as if she'd never been surer of anything in her life. "Oh, yeah. He has all the signs. All these projects he does for her? Mowing her lawn? The towel bar? Please. Any excuse to hang around here. He's drawn to her like a moth to a flame. I can't believe I didn't figure it out before."

"What should we do?"

"We'll have to put out the flame. Duh."

"She's dead, Angel. That pretty much puts out the flame. I mean what are we going to do about him coming around? He told me he'll come every weekend to mow and take the renters' garbage. How long before he gets suspicious about not seeing her?"

Angel thought for a minute. "I know," she said at last.

"We'll give her a boyfriend."

The image of Louise's lolling off her recliner flashed in front of me. "That might be kind of hard at this stage," I said.

"No," Angel said. "That'll be easy. But first we'd better get her buried."

9

George had dug three big holes in a row for us. Angel and I got to work shoveling out the earth between them. Twenty minutes later, we stood panting over a trench that was maybe two feet deep. We climbed down into it and set to work again. The ground became sandier, but loaded with rocks. After half an hour of solid digging, stopping only to wipe sweat and swat gnats, I thought the pit looked enough like a grave.

"Another foot deeper," Angel insisted. "I'm telling you, that goat . . ."

More digging. The mound beside us grew. Finally, just

as the sun began to fall toward the tree line, Angel dropped her shovel. "Let's go get that pumpkin."

We climbed out of the pit and went in.

"Well," Angel said. She didn't take a step into the den, though.

"Well," I said. I grabbed the Febreze and gave Louise another good spraying, but I didn't go in either. I stood next to Angel, trying to judge how heavy my great-aunt might be. She wasn't tall, but whenever she heaved herself out of a chair, you could tell there was a lot of effort involved.

Angel made two fists and pumped her arms, like a wrestler. She dropped them and sighed.

"Right," I said. We stood there some more.

"This is ridiculous," Angel said. She marched into the room and went behind Louise's recliner and gave it a shove. "Well, I can move her," she said. "But I can't look at her." She pulled the throw from the back of the couch and flung it over Louise.

It made all the difference, not having to look at what had happened to Louise. I joined Angel behind the recliner, and together we pushed it to the doorway. We steered Louise down the hall and into the kitchen—it was surprisingly easy, and I thought, Well, there's a nice benefit to keeping your floors waxed. I kept this to myself, of course.

And then there we were at the back door. Which the recliner was too wide for.

"I've got an idea," Angel said.

She left, and I stayed with Louise. Even though she was under the throw and couldn't have seen anything, and even though she was dead, for heaven's sake, I was glad that her last view on earth was of the golden light of sunset pouring over those blueberry bushes she was so proud of. I liked it that there was a pot of chili simmering beside her in her own neat kitchen. "This is what you want, too, isn't it? You didn't want us to call the police and be taken away, right?" I was surprised to find that it didn't feel weird to talk to a dead person. I only wished she could answer.

I gave the chili a stir, then turned the flame down even lower. "Probably not as good as yours," I admitted.

I heard the scrape of furniture being moved, and then Angel was back, dragging the braided rug from the den. "Her magic carpet," she explained. We tugged the chair back enough to unroll the rug out on the step.

Angel and I looked at each other. She bent to Louise's feet and gestured that I should get her arms. We turned our heads and tried not to breathe.

"One . . . two . . . *three*," she counted.

And we heaved.

For a minute, it looked like we'd overshot and Louise

would go tumbling over the steps. But she rocked back onto her side, and Angel and I let out our breaths. We stepped over her and each grabbed an edge of rug and tugged her off the landing. "Sorry," I whispered at each bump.

The path through the middle of the garden was fairly smooth, but it wasn't designed to drag a body down. It took both of us straining together to make any progress at all, and within minutes we were dripping with sweat and gasping for breath. The mosquitoes came out and decided this was just how they liked their dinner.

After what seemed like an hour of dragging, we reached the trench. "One, two, *three*," Angel called again. We took one edge of the rug and lifted. Louise wobbled at the lip for a minute, as if she were having second thoughts about all this, but then with an extra push we sent her rolling softly into the pit, her jewelry making tiny jangles as it slid in with her. We dropped the rug in, and it fell over her with a hushed thud.

I turned to the heaps of fresh earth behind me, and my arms went numb.

Not Angel. She filled a shovel with dirt and tossed it into the grave without looking. And then another and another.

I touched Angel's arm. "Hold on." I went inside and looked around Louise's room for something that I could bury with her. I settled on the picture of her with my grandmother, the one with the tarnished frame. I went back out and knelt beside the grave and dropped it in.

"What's that for?" Angel asked.

"I don't know," I admitted. "Company, I guess."

After that, I could cover her up. It was hard work. We shoveled and raked, but that hole didn't seem to get any fuller for the longest time. At least when true evening fell, the mosquitoes gave up, but by then we were covered with bites under the sweat and dirt.

At last the grave was filled. We piled the rest of the dirt up into three smooth mounds over where George had dug the holes. Angel raked the seaweed around the mounds. Then she brushed her hands together as if she was finished. "Let's go eat some chili," she said.

"We can't just go in, Angel. We have to say something."

Angel turned back to the grave with her hands on her hips. "Jeez, I hope she's deep enough," she said. "Otherwise, every dog in Barnstable County . . ."

"Not like that! Something to lay her to rest."

"Why do we have to say anything? We're not really burying her, not that way. This is temporary, Stella."

"Temporary?"

"When your mom gets here, we'll have to explain things. And then people will come, and . . . do whatever. Right?"

I realized I hadn't wanted to think about that part, but

I nodded. "I guess." But it didn't feel right. "No. She and my grandmother only had one brother, and he was killed in Vietnam. There's no one else to do this. We have to say something."

"Fine," said Angel. She nodded over the fresh dirt. "Rest in peace. I hope you . . . you know . . . rest in peace."

"Not *to* her, Angel! You say something *about* her. Something good you remember about the person. Don't you know anything about funerals?"

Too late I realized what my mean, cramped-hearted self had said. Angel knew a lot about funerals.

Angel glared at me, fury gathering up like a volcano. "Who put you in charge of everything?" she spat. "I didn't know her. I don't have any good memories of her. She didn't care about me, and I didn't care about her. She's yours— you say something!" She stormed off down the path and disappeared into the house with a door slam.

Suddenly, it was so quiet there in the darkening garden, with just a few chirping crickets and the soft rustle of oak leaves beside me. The yellow light spilling from the house seemed to beckon me inside, but the thought of comfort made me feel guilty.

I turned back to the dark mounds of earth. The grave; it was a grave now. I shuddered at how real that word made things. Under this dirt was the body of my great-aunt. A real person who had been alive just two days ago. She'd had no idea this was coming; she was just planning on a regular day doing regular things. She had punched the microwave extra hard in front of me Friday morning but then thought about things and dredged up a good memory of my mother and promised to teach me how to make a pie. She had packed us lunches and sent us off to school and stirred cream into her coffee and thought, Good, now I've got an hour with the *Today* show before I have to start my chores, and then had never made it back into her kitchen to put that cream away.

She had been a real person, and now she was really dead. What made that seem the saddest was that Angel had been right—we had never really known her. I had no good memories to share either.

I thought back to my grandmother's service, to how many people had stood up and told stories about her and said how much she had meant to them.

"I'm sorry I didn't try harder to find any connections between us," I whispered into the quiet. "I'm sorry about everything, about you dying—I hope that didn't hurt. I didn't know about your heart. I wish you'd told me. I'm sorry I didn't carry all those bags for you—maybe if I had . . . Well, I'm sorry about you having to be out here like this. But at least it's in your garden, near your blueberries."

I looked over at them then: dozens of bushes that even in the dark were ripening up their berries for Louise's blue-ribbon pies. And then I knew just what to say.

I faced the bushes as though they were a crowd of mourners. "When I first got here, I looked out at this backyard from my bedroom window, and I didn't think much of it. The ground was brown and scruffy, and all that grew for a lawn were a few patches of tough grass that were brown and scruffy, too. It looked to me as if the world's biggest mangy dog had laid himself out back to catch a little sun, with more bald patches than fur. You wouldn't see a yard like this in *House and Garden* magazine, that's all I'm saying."

I glanced up at the house, hoping that Angel would hear me and change her mind and come out. She didn't, so after a minute, I went on.

"But Louise was always out here doing something, and when she was inside, she was reading gardening magazines. Friday she told me about her blueberry bushes, and how proud she was of them. Of you. She kept pictures of her pies on her refrigerator, did you know that? I figure someone who cared that much about growing things was a good person." Then I said "Amen," because even though my mother never let me set foot in a church, I knew that much.

I started to head in. But something about those blueberry

bushes, huddled together in the darkness, made me pause.

I was nine when my grandmother died, old enough to read the obituary in the newspaper. *She leaves behind a daughter, Margot, and a beloved granddaughter, Stella.* I'd stared at our names in print and felt exposed, as though our left-behindness was a shame on public view. At the funeral, I imagined everyone was seeing us that way. Her left-behinds.

These blueberry bushes. They were Louise's left-behinds. Without her, they were probably going to become a wild tangle; then after a while they'd stop growing. They'd wilt, and shrivel up, and die.

I knew how it felt when the one person tending you disappeared.

"Louise asked me to help her take care of you. She's gone, so I guess it's all up to me now. You are my *destino*, or whatever Angel said the word was. My destiny," I promised out loud. "You can count on me."

Inside, I found Angel hunched over a mug full of chili. I ran water and squirted dish soap over my hands. "Um . . . Angel?"

Angel raised a warning palm to me without looking up.

"Rewind, okay? I'm sorry. That was a dumb thing I said."

"The phone's on the counter. Call someone who cares."

I dried my hands and sat down across from her.

She got up and slammed her mug down next to the stove. "We just have to survive the summer without getting caught," she said, her words thrown over her shoulder. "This isn't an episode of *Friends*. Got it?" She slapped some more chili into the mug, letting it spatter over the counter, then left the room with it.

I looked over at the phone. I did want to call someone who cared. But I didn't know who that could be. I put the chili in the refrigerator without eating any, because my stomach hurt.

People's sleeping sounds are like fingerprints.

Louise had been easy to keep track of. Her snoring was loud and steady, except for when she snorted herself awake every now and then. My grandmother had been a steady snorer, too, but it was a soft, easy whuffling. My mother—who was the reason I learned to listen in the first place—didn't make any breathing sounds at all, but she whimpered all night, as if in her dreams someone was always being a little mean to her.

Angel didn't snore or whimper, but every once in a while I'd hear a small, quick rustling of the sheets. I somehow knew she was scissoring her feet around, like a dog with a dream. I'd sit up in my bed, straining to hear it over Louise's snoring, and then when I did, I'd lie back again thinking, That girl's here, but she wants to run.

The night we buried Louise, I woke up around midnight as usual and lay still, listening for Angel's rustle. What I heard instead was rain. It took a minute to remember what had happened earlier in the night. I lay in my bed for as long as I could, trying not to imagine the rain washing away the dirt we'd shoveled over Louise. That was crazy, that couldn't happen. But then I gave up and went over to the window.

A full moon lit the backyard silver, so bright the trees threw clear shadows on the ground. But I still *heard* rain— not a soft, gentle rain, but a sharp pattering that made me shiver. I lifted the screen and stuck my hand out to be sure: It was not raining. I listened harder; now the sound was more like chewing—the sound a million angry bees might make if they had sharp teeth. I looked over to the garden, to the fresh, dark mounds of dirt over Louise.

I ran back to my bed and crushed a pillow to each ear.

When Angel came downstairs Monday morning, ten minutes before the bus was due, she glared at me as though it was my fault school started at eight. "You know how to drive?" she asked, plunking herself down next to me at the kitchen table.

"Of course not." I slid the Cheerios over to her.

Angel pitched the box of cereal over her shoulder and into the sink, pulled a Dum Dum out of her pocket, and stuck it in her mouth. She started talking around it. "We're going to have to learn, then. We'll start today."

"What?"

"Well, how else are we going to get around?"

"No! For one thing, it's illegal. For another . . . Never mind, the bus is coming."

"I don't even know why we're bothering to go to school," Angel muttered.

"Yes, you do. So no one gets suspicious. We decided it last night. *Both* of us." I got up to wash out my bowl and spoon—Heloise says cleanup's easier when you attack it right away. I lifted the Cheerios box and was relieved that only a few Os were dissolving in the sink. I closed up the box and put it back in the cupboard, then leaned into the window. Louise's garden was shining bright and green and innocent under the early sun, with its dark secret hidden deep underneath. "Are we really doing this?" I wasn't sure if I'd said the words aloud.

Angel made a scoffing sound and hoisted her backpack. "Don't talk to anyone today."

Like I would. I picked up my stuff and followed her out, feeling a sick worry pool in my belly. As Bus Two came growling down Pine Lane, I remembered. "Angel, did you hear anything last night?"

"Like what?"

"Like a chewing sound. Like . . . something bad."

Angel shot me one of her looks. "I didn't hear anything." Then she snapped her earphones on and looked away. On the bus, she took a seat as far away from me as possible. As if I had something contagious.

Wherever that girl was, I wasn't. I could do that again.

School, at least, was easy. Nobody seemed to notice the big sign I felt sure I wore, the one that flashed, ASK ME ABOUT MY WEEKEND! The teachers were preoccupied with collecting books and recording grades in their ledgers, their faces grim as they pressed their red pencils along to the finish line. The kids were pretty much on vacation already, and neither Angel nor I had made any friends—when you arrive at the end of a school year, the groups are already tied into hard knots. Angel and I ate lunch at opposite sides of the loners' table without talking. Same as usual.

I spent my afternoon study hall in the library, and I never even saw the librarian. This was a relief, because as soon as I'd arrived in April, Ms. Richardson had decided to make me a project of hers. She seemed to be able to read my mind. She'd suggest a story about a girl having trouble making friends in a new school just when I was feeling the loneliest, or a book about families getting back together when I was most worried about my mother not coming back. I know it sounds crazy, but I wouldn't have been surprised if Ms. Richardson had handed me a book about kids burying people in their backyards.

*   *   *

When I got off the bus, I remembered to collect the mail so the postman wouldn't get suspicious. There was a lot, since it hadn't been picked up since Thursday. Junk mostly. Coupons for gutter cleaning and picture framing, real estate flyers. I almost missed it: Stuck inside a Humane Society brochure was a postcard from my mother.

The Grand Canyon.

Hi, Stella. I'll have to bring you here someday—it's amazing! Off to California tomorrow! A theater director I used to know is looking for a costume designer . . . me! Hope you're having fun with Louise. . . . How's the beach? Love, Mom.

Hope you're having fun? How's the beach? Like we were both just on some summer vacation? Part of me wanted to rip up the postcard and throw it away. But I reread the line about work and thought that a costume designer sounded more promising than a "possible" job with horses. Then I tucked the postcard back inside the brochure with the sad-faced puppies and wedged it into the bottom of the mail basket.

When Angel came in, I showed her the bills—electric and phone. "Should we open them?"

"What's the point? We aren't paying them."

"What if they shut off the service?"

Angel dropped a couple of slices of bread in the toaster. "So we pay them. You know how?"

I shrugged yes. Over the past two years, I'd had to learn. Still. "Forgery's a crime, you know."

Angel smirked and rolled her eyes toward the garden.

She had a point.

I fished Louise's checkbook out of the drawer and sat down with it. She was as neat with it as she was with her kitchen, so right away I could see that she'd paid all her bills about a week ago, on the fifteenth. I saw something else: There were no checks written that could have been rent, and there were none written to a bank that could have been mortgage payments. That meant she owned this house all right, free and clear. Then I ran down her deposits, to see how long the money might last. The amount marked "Foster Care" surprised me.

"Angel," I said, "how much did you say the state pays for having you?"

"Like seventeen bucks a day. Why?"

I did the math. Louise had been getting paid for me, too.

I tossed the checkbook back in the drawer as if it had just bitten me and tore the bills in half. "They always send a second notice," I said. Another thing I'd learned over the past year. "So we're safe for a month at least."

"Good," Angel said. She opened the refrigerator door. "We're out of milk."

The last three days of school passed. As soon as I got off the bus each afternoon, I went straight out to the garden and got to work. I told Angel I was doing it so things would look normal. But the real reason was that I had promised those plants I would. And I figured I owed Louise that much. She had given us her home. She was still giving us her home. It came with some responsibilities.

I found out I liked gardening. Plucking weeds from the even lines of vegetables soothed me the way cleaning did. When the weeds were out, I smoothed the dirt around each stem, just like you'd smooth a blanket around a sleeping baby. I planted the tray of seedlings Louise had bought back on Thursday, and watered them gently. After a couple of days, they straightened up and began to throw out shiny new leaves. That made me proud.

The blueberry bushes were another story, though. I raked in the fertilizer and spread the mulch, following directions in Louise's gardening books. I ran buckets of water out to them, since the hose didn't reach that far, and even brought out a spray bottle to mist them. Nothing helped—they got droopier each day.

"I give up!" I yelled finally, kneeling in the middle of the patch, yanking weeds. "What do you want?" I glanced back at the house and saw Angel watching me from her open window. I jumped to my feet, embarrassed. But then I waved up at Angel. Because, so what? She wasn't talking to me; so what if I talked to plants?

The outside world didn't bother us much that week, and we returned the favor. No one stopped by, and most of the phone calls came in while we were at school, so the machine caught them. The library letting Louise know her book was in. Some guy running for some office, hoping he could count on her vote. A bunch of people calling about the cottages. Except for Plover the first week, we were fully booked, so we didn't call them back.

The first time the phone rang at night, we jumped. Louise wouldn't pay for caller ID—"Why would I pay good money to find out who's calling me two seconds earlier than they're gonna tell me themselves?" was her thought—so there was no way to know if it was safe to answer.

"We should pick up," Angel decided. "So no one gets suspicious." Then she waved her arm toward the phone to let me know that "we" meant "me."

It was Anita, someone who went to bingo with Louise.

I mouthed B-I-N-G-O to Angel. Angel pantomimed hanging up.

I couldn't. How could I have forgotten about bingo? It was the highlight of Louise's month! My mouth went into its nervous blabbing spree. "She's out shopping. She's out shopping for us. For food. She likes to get us our favorite foods."

Angel sank to the kitchen table and made a face, as if I was the lamest liar she'd ever heard.

"I've got company, so I won't be there next time," Anita said. "I'll see her in August, though. I wonder if you could give her the message, dear."

"No junk food, though," I assured Anita. "I want two healthy girls, that's what she's always saying."

Angel threw her hands up in the air, as if I was such a loser, she gave up.

Even then I couldn't stop. "We're all really healthy here!"

Angel jumped from the table and made a slashing motion across her neck.

"Well, gotta go," I said.

Angel took the phone from me. "From now on, I answer it," she said.

So the days passed—school and then gardening and then scrounging up a meal with Angel. But the nights didn't.

I'd lie in bed and I'd hear things. Coyotes, howling in the distance about a kill; great blue herons screeching like strangled cats; mice in the eaves. Little shifts and creaks that I knew were only the normal house sounds, sounds I'd slept right through when Louise was here, but now they scared me so much, my heart knocked against the mattress.

The worst sound of all was the chewing. The sound I couldn't help imagining was Louise's new night sound— her new fingerprint. I'd asked Angel again if she'd heard it, and she snapped at me that she didn't know what I was talking about.

One night in the middle of the week it hit me, so hard I jerked bolt upright, shaking. Crazy people heard sounds that weren't there.

Or people who felt guilty about things.

CHAPTER

◇ 11 ◇

Friday morning, no more school. As soon as I got up, I went into Louise's room. I didn't like it in there, surrounded by her things with their wilted-floweriness, but I'd searched everywhere else for links to my mother. And I found one as soon as I stepped inside: Holding the closet door open was an iron doorstop in the shape of a pug dog. It was identical to one that had been at my grandmother's house—they must have been a pair once. I had loved that dog. He always sat at the kitchen door, looking over his shoulder as if to say, Come on in, I'm holding it open for you. I used to carry him all around with me when I was little, like he was a real dog, although he probably weighed almost as much as I did.

My mother had hated that doorstop, though. She'd stub her toe on it and curse, time after time when she was pacing around. After my grandmother died, she'd gotten rid of it.

I bent down and patted the pug's head, and then I went into Louise's closet. The first box I pulled down was full of Christmas ornaments. A memory sprang up.

A New Year's Day. My mother had been gone since Christmas this time. My grandmother and I were taking down the tree. Snow was falling outside, and inside it was too quiet, with my mother gone. All that silence sounded like blame to me—as if it was telling me I'd done something to make my mother leave. "Why didn't you make her stay?" I asked my grandmother. "You're her mother. Why don't you tell her what to do?"

My grandmother lifted an ornament from the tree—a glass ball, sheer as ice water, with gold threads shivering through it.

"This is your mother, Stella," my grandmother said, holding up the ornament. "You and I are rubber balls. You drop us, we bounce. But your mother needs to be handled carefully, packed in cotton. It's my fault, I know that. When her father left us, I decided nothing should hurt her again. She was so young when she had you—just a child herself, really. I'm afraid I protected her too much, made excuses for her. I'm sorry about that now, but I can't change it."

I burrowed into her soft shoulder, sorry for being such a baby. I'd understood what she was telling me. But I'd seen something else, too: That ornament was beautiful. A rubber ball was plain.

I closed the box, and that was the end of my poking around Louise's closet. I picked up the pug doorstop and carried him to my room and put him down gently. "Welcome to your new home."

Then I went downstairs. Angel was watching television. "Maybe I'll go to the beach," I said.

I was really just trying out the idea, but Angel looked relieved. "Whatever," she said. "Just don't talk to anyone."

I made a couple of peanut butter sandwiches and filled a bottle with water, then hurried into my suit, grabbed a book and a towel, and headed out.

The parking-lot asphalt was hot and sticky under my flip-flops. I hurried to the water and started to walk east. Every couple of hundred yards, a big rock jetty stuck out like a barnacled arm into the sea, dividing the shore into a dozen calm-water coves. I kept going, each cove getting less crowded, stopping now and then to pick up shells—broken ones only, to remind myself of what George had said.

When I reached the last cove, I dumped my stuff, peeled

off my T-shirt, and marched into the water. The cold was a shock, but a good one. I walked out until the water was waist high, and then I plunged in.

I swam in the salty, face-slapping waves until my body was tired, then spread out my towel at the base of the far jetty and flopped down. And for the first time since burying Louise, there was no angry chewing sound when I closed my eyes.

I woke up with a little headache and a stinging sunburn on my back, but calmer than I'd felt in a week. A group of high school girls had settled at the other end of my cove while I'd slept. Their laughter drifted over me with the breeze. I adjusted my book and sunglasses so I could watch them.

Even without hearing their words, I knew they were talking about things like nail polish and boys and summer plans. None of them had buried someone in their backyard, none of them were living a big lie, like Angel and I were. But then it struck me: If those girls looked over at me, they'd just see a plain-looking eleven-year-old reading a book. They'd never suspect the secret I was hiding. I looked up and down the beach and wondered if maybe everyone could be hiding some big secret. I sank into the warm sand, smiling at the idea of a beach full of people, tied together by their secret-hiding.

I took my time walking home, and when I climbed up the path and into the clearing before our backyard, I stopped to check on the blueberry bushes. They looked even scruffier than before, the leaves crumpled and dull. The berries seemed to have stopped getting bigger.

I had done everything the gardening books said to do. These bushes were watered and fed and weeded, and the weather had been perfect. And then I realized—if plants could grieve, this is how they would look. They were missing Louise, the same way I missed my grandmother when she died. What I'd missed most was her just sitting with me while I did my homework, or watched a show, or read. Just her being beside me.

I flattened the witchgrass and plucked out some stones and then lay down among the bushes. I tried to imagine what Louise might say if she were out here beside them. Probably something about pies. Maybe something about bringing them down to the diner, or winning another blue ribbon. I tried to hear her voice in my head—it had seemed to me Louise was always grumbling—but when I finally did, she wasn't talking about pies. "Puh. There's nobody else?" I heard her ask. "All right, I'll take her in. As long as it's seventeen dollars a day."

Just then, a screen door banged open. Jolted, I rolled

over and lifted my head.

Angel stood on the back steps, holding a kitchen chair to her chest. She swung around as if she was checking to see if the coast was clear. I ducked back down. I didn't hear anything for a while, so very carefully, I lifted my head.

Angel carried the chair down the middle path of the garden. She stopped at the end and set it down right next to where Louise was buried, and settled the legs into the dirt. Then she sat down and looked all around again. I held still.

"I watched your show for you," I heard her say. "That Elaina is up to no good. She's not really pregnant—did you know that? But here's the real news: Yesterday ended with a stranger showing up out of the blue at Mrs. Hartford's door, and all we saw was his back and how shocked Mrs. Hartford was when she saw him there, like she was seeing a ghost. Well, guess who he is? Her son! The one who's been gone all these years and everybody thought was dead! Turns out he was in some secret spy operation and then he had amnesia. So now, look out, he's back—and the worst part is, he thinks he's still married."

Angel described every scene. One woman was pregnant but telling everyone she wasn't. Another woman wasn't pregnant but telling people she was. Men told women they didn't love them when they did, and vice versa. Apparently, the main thing soap opera characters did was lie to each other.

Angel wrapped it up, then promised she'd watch every day. I heard her clunk the chair up the steps and inside the kitchen door, but I lay there with the blueberry bushes for a while. When I finally went back inside, Angel was watching television.

I stuck my head in the doorway, all casual. "What've you been doing?"

Angel jerked a shoulder to the television set, as if my question was too ridiculous to bother answering.

I went back into the kitchen and checked the chairs, just to make sure I hadn't imagined it. No, one of them had fresh dirt socks on. That girl was a mystery.

CHAPTER · 12 ·

Saturday morning, the phone rang and I jumped up. The court deal was that my mother would call once a week. I'd asked her to try for Saturday mornings, so I'd be sure to be there. She'd missed half of them so far, it was true, but now here she was, Saturday morning. And I had so much to tell her.

Except it wasn't her. Just someone asking about a vacancy in August. "Sorry," I said, and hung up hard.

I turned toward the southwest, where I figured my mother was. *Please call*, I willed into the air. I'd read that people who are really connected can hear each other's thoughts sometimes. *Please call. I need you.*

And the phone rang!

But no, it was only George. "I'm heading out soon—tide's in an hour. Just wanted to make sure you're all ready. Check-in's at three. Probably everybody will show up right on the dot—people don't like to lose a minute of vacation, you see."

"Louise isn't worried," I told him. Which was the truth, at least.

"Well, I'll come by next weekend for the trash. You need anything before then, you just—"

"We won't need anything," I said, a little sharper than I'd meant to.

The line was quiet for a minute. And then George asked, "Are you all right?"

"Fine," I said. Which was a really big lie. "I have to go now."

At quarter of three, Angel and I parked ourselves on the grass under the LINGER LONGER sign. I had the master key, and Angel held Louise's planner, which listed who went in which cottage when.

"It's going to be okay," I said, twisting the key around my finger. "Louise broke her ankle. We're here to let everyone in. That's all."

"Sure," Angel agreed. I could tell she didn't believe it any more than I did.

Five minutes later, a blue SUV with a New York license plate pulled in. Big as it was, it still looked ready to burst with vacation stuff—bikes and boogie boards and fishing poles on the rack above; suitcases and coolers and beach chairs pressed against the back windows. Two red-haired boys about five or six burst out first, followed by a woman who got out and did some stretches as her sons chased each other around with the badminton racquets.

"Here we go," the woman sighed as her husband unfolded himself.

"Here we go," I said to Angel. We got up and headed for the car, and just then a second SUV—this one with Ohio plates—crunched up over the shell driveway. From it spilled two more kids—a boy around seven and a tiny little girl, each of them with a cloud of black curls and overalls on. And a third car, an old white Volvo wagon, pulled in before we'd even said hello to the first family.

For the next hour and a half, Angel and I didn't stop. We told everyone that Louise was sorry not to meet them, but she'd just broken her ankle and so we were in charge. Nobody raised an eyebrow. We opened all the cottages except Plover and showed the three families around and answered a million questions and ran back and forth to the supply shed for charcoal and grill lighters and extra lawn chairs and croquet mallets.

After the first big rush, Angel and I set ourselves up at the picnic table in our backyard, where everyone could see us in case they needed something. I thumbed through one of Louise's gardening magazines, and Angel lay back with her earphones on. One by one, the families drove out—to show their kids the ocean, to find the center of town, or to pick up groceries for dinner, I guessed. But by the time evening fell, they were all back. The parents lit grills and cracked open beers and sprayed bug repellent and turned on radios. The kids ran around checking out the cottages and each other. Within half an hour, you'd think they'd grown up together.

When the first hot dogs and hamburgers began to sizzle on the grills, Angel and I went in. We warmed up some tomato soup and spread peanut butter over the last of the crackers. Afterward, I went upstairs. I lay on my bed with my fists bunched under my chin and looked down over the cottages. There was something magic about them, the way they seemed to make everyone so happy. The kids hollered and chased each other through the yellow parallelograms of spilled window light. The parents laughed together quietly and then, at the same time, called their kids in. Magic.

A half-moon rose in the sky. The scent of burnt

marshmallows sweetened the air. And an emptiness welled up inside me. It felt like hunger, but it wasn't in my stomach. I wondered if Angel, in the next bedroom, was watching the families, too. I wondered if her heart felt like it was clenching around nothing.

By noon on Sunday, all three families had packed up their sunscreened kids, their coolers and rafts and towels, and headed out to begin their vacations.

Angel and I stood at the window and looked out at the empty, silent yard.

"Now what?" I asked.

Angel shrugged. "Now nothing. Until they get back. Just normal life."

Normal life. My old life, with my mother the past two years, hadn't even been close to normal. I'd been to four different schools while we bounced around Cape Cod, and there'd been a couple of months in Oregon when I'd barely even been inside a classroom. The last time I'd had a normal life had been when we'd lived with my grandmother, and now that time seemed so far away, I was already forgetting it. This was my life now. I was a manager of the Linger Longer Cottage Colony.

As weird as it sounds, that first week there were renters, we fell into a routine. I'd get up early and make coffee, so the kitchen would smell like a grown-up was living there. I'd turn on the morning news Louise used to watch and open the curtains at nine the way Louise had, and pretty soon the renters would start banging on the screen door.

Once, Louise had told me that the hardest part of her job was answering their questions. Actually, the way she put it wasn't that nice. "Puh," she'd said. "Those tourists must sit around all day thinking up ridiculous questions to bother me with."

She was right about the number of questions, but I didn't think they were ridiculous. Sometimes it was a little kid, puffed with pride that he'd been trusted with such an important mission, but usually it was a parent. The adults always looked a little uncomfortable in their vacation clothes. The men, especially, couldn't seem to decide if they should wear socks or not, and kept looking down at their bare legs as if it was a shock to see their own knees.

I noticed that the mother from Tern glanced around the kitchen while she was talking, like she was judging Louise by how she kept her house. Because of that, I made sure to clean things up right away, the way she would have.

Once in a while, someone would ask how Louise was doing with her broken ankle. I wasn't a very good liar, so I came up with some tricky answers. "She's keeping off it," I'd say. "She's not complaining." They never asked anything more, just went right into the reason they'd come over. "What's a good beach for kids?" or "Where can we get a beach sticker?" And always a question about tides—after all, if you lived in a city in the middle of the country, how would you know that the tides go in and out twice a day, about an hour later each day? It made me happy, not irritated, to answer them.

Besides the questions, there were the emergencies. Every day, someone needed something right away—a raft repaired, a drawer unstuck, a rusted umbrella opened. "Stay right here," I'd say. "I'll run up and ask Louise about that."

And I'd run upstairs all right, but it was Heloise I asked for advice.

One of the twins got a splinter in his heel his parents couldn't get with tweezers. Heloise and I saved the day by taping a clove of garlic over it—the garlic drew the splinter out in a few hours. When Mr. Gull came complaining about a clogged sink, I found a hint about pouring a bottle of soda down the drain. Heloise never let me down.

Finally, with all the questions answered and emergencies solved, the families left for whatever they were doing that day, and I was free to go to the garden to work.

That got harder every day. Louise hadn't marked her rows, so I had to figure out what each plant was before I could even begin to take care of it. And she'd apparently gone on a planting spree the week before she died—I'd look at a nice empty patch of garden one day, and the next there'd be a fringe of green lace poking up in a line, asking to be attended to. The best I could do about that was to yank up the things that weren't growing in a clear row, and hope they were weeds.

On the bright side, the vegetables were doing pretty well. The zucchini flowers were curling back to reveal miniature squashes. The tomatoes were green, but some were the size of golf balls. The peas had climbed all over the twigs Louise had stuck in the ground for them, and looked like they were slapping each other high fives for busting out of their seeds into such a great garden.

The blueberry bushes, though, were getting worse. According to Louise's gardening books, they should be thick with shiny, green, oval leaves and dotted with berries starting to turn blue. Instead, the leaves looked more frayed each day, and the berries had definitely stopped growing.

I raked more mulch around them, watered them, and pulled more weeds. I started hoeing in the morning's coffee grounds when I figured out why Louise had saved them: I read that it made the soil more acid, the way blueberries liked it. I worked until I was sweaty and tired every morning, but nothing helped. I had promised to take care of them, and I was failing.

By noon each day, I would give up. I'd drag on a bathing suit, scrounge up something to eat, and head down the path to the beach.

I felt better when I got there. I don't know what it is about a beach—the drifty, fake-coconut scent of suntan lotion, the endless *whoosh* of little waves lapping the shore, or the way the sun beats down so bright and hot, you feel too baked to think—but when I was there, I could almost forget everything. I floated in the cool water, too tired to actually swim, then flopped down on a towel and read. I read a lot. Louise hardly had any books to choose from— she used to say she liked her stories on the tube—but I found a set of *Reader's Digest* Condensed Books in her bedroom, and those kept me going.

Although what I found out was this: The books were abridged, which I figured meant the *Reader's Digest* people put in little bridges between what they decided were the good parts, cutting out whatever they decided was boring. The problem was, what if the *Reader's Digest* people and I didn't agree about what parts were boring? Most people would probably say, go right for the action: people fighting and chasing each other, or kissing, or lying about things. But my favorite parts were different. I liked it when two characters were getting to know each other. Just talking. It was best if they were inside a house, and the author spent a little time describing the room, so I could feel like I was there, too, sipping cocoa and watching the curtains billow in and out.

What I did about the *Reader's Digest* problem was this: Whenever I came to a part that looked like something might be missing, I made up something I'd like to be there. And I started to think, lying out there on my towel in the sun, that maybe I'd make a good author. One thing about any books I'd write—you would be reading about the cleaning-up parts of scenes. It drives me crazy how characters are always making messes and then the author doesn't tell about cleaning them up. Everybody eats dinner in books, but nobody does the dishes. People wrestle around in the mud and have accidents with blood, and nobody does the laundry. I just hate that.

The other thing I did out there on the beach was watch people. It's easy to do behind sunglasses. There were loads of families, old couples reading newspapers, and groups of teenagers working on suntans, but what I liked best were the clammers.

They came at low tide and they worked on their hands and knees, digging dark holes into the sandbars, their wire baskets filling up beside them. Now and then one of them would sit back on his heels and call out something and the others would laugh; I never caught the words, but I liked it that they were teasing each other, making the time pass. Spinning their strands.

I got to recognize the clammers after a couple of days—mostly they were grown men, but there was one boy. He was almost as tall as the men but only about thirteen or fourteen, and he had ragged cutoffs and messy, sun-bleached hair. He stayed to himself, and every time I looked over, his shoulders were working steadily as he pitched clam after clam into his basket. When he finished working a hole, he filled it back in with sand, even though the next high tide would take care of that in a few hours. I understood that; I would do that, too. I wished I could tell the clammer boy that, but Angel had made me promise not to talk to anyone.

Angel. She was back to barely grunting at me, but every afternoon she had a chatty little soap opera review with Louise. I'd time my return from the beach for when she'd be watching the show, then go upstairs, pretending I wanted a nap. At four, when Angel went out to give her report, I hung at the window to listen. Not much happened in that soap opera. Day after day, the characters just lied about the same stuff. But I liked the way Angel put things.

"That Elaina! What's she thinking anyway? Like her husband isn't going to notice one day? 'Hey, honey, that's a *pillow* you've got under your dress!'"

Angel was starting to get involved with the show herself. "Poor Mrs. Hartford!" she went on one day, and you could tell she meant it. "Wouldn't you think she'd get a little time to enjoy the fact that her son's back from the dead? But no. They call her the heart of Spring Valley, but really, she's more like the woe bank—all the characters dump their troubles on her and go trotting off, leaving her holding a bucket full of misery. Today her niece called, all hysterical because her fiancé is in love with someone else. . . ."

So that was the weekday routine: helping the renters, working in the garden, going to the beach, and listening to Angel's visits with Louise. In the late afternoons, the renters would get back and their questions would start again—not as many as in the mornings, but always a few. In the evenings, Angel and I watched television—Louise only got the basic channels and there was nothing good on because it was summer, but it kept me from what I dreaded the most. Finally, though, I'd have to go to bed.

And try not to hear the sound that wasn't there.

CHAPTER
◇ 14 ◇

We ran out of food that week. On Tuesday, I looked into the refrigerator and found it was empty—really, truly empty. The coffee cake was in the freezer, and it was going to stay there. There were still a few things in the cupboard, but they were the kinds of things people picked up on the spur of the moment and then later looked at and wondered what the heck they'd been thinking. Anchovy paste. Dried mushrooms. A jar of capers, which looked and tasted like little sour olives. Just looking in those cupboards made my stomach twist over to gnaw on itself.

I carried the rest of the hurricane food up from the

cellar, except for the Crisco—what would anyone want with Crisco, anyway? My first instinct was to ration it out, figure out how much of what things we should eat each day and explain it to Angel. But I remembered Angel snapping at me about my rules, and suddenly, I was sick of them too.

I picked a lettuce and a handful of pea pods from the garden, baked the tiny ham with both cans of baked beans, and made the cornbread mix into muffins. Angel pushed the green stuff off her plate, but she ate everything else. We emptied our plates and filled them again. When we were finished, I gave Angel the bad news.

"What do you mean 'out of food'?" she asked.

"I mean the leftovers here will feed us tomorrow. There's still one can of tomato soup. There's a stick of butter in the freezer. Oh, some maple syrup. And that's all."

"So now what?"

"We go to the store."

Angel's face broke into a hopeful smile. I followed her gaze to Louise's car keys hanging by the door.

"No," I said firmly. "We walk."

Angel gaped at me. "It's got to be ten miles away!"

"Maybe five," I said. "And five back, carrying groceries. But we have to do it."

Angel poked around in her pocket and fished out a Dum Dum. She got up, laid the lollipop on the cutting board, and sawed it in half. She gave me the half with the stick. "Now we're out of food," she said.

The next day, we emptied Louise's bingo money out of her Earl Grey tea tin and left. As we stepped outside, the sunlight actually seemed to flare, as if someone had clicked the brightness dial up a notch. It made me wish I was wearing a ski mask.

"Act normal," Angel said, so I figured she was feeling overexposed, too.

We set out, sweating from almost the first step. Angel wasn't in the mood for talking, but every once in a while, she'd try out a grocery list.

"Lasagna. With garlic bread. And I want some cookies."

"We'd be lucky to get one meal's worth out of eleven dollars."

"And seventy cents."

"Huh? Oh, fine . . . eleven dollars and seventy cents. It's not much, Angel. With that little money, you have to stick with the basics."

"How come you know this stuff, anyway?"

"I just do." Because if I hadn't figured out how to stretch grocery money, my mother and I would have starved.

"How about hot dogs and chips? Those have to be cheap."

"Better," I said. "Maybe three meals."

She pulled ahead of me and growled over her shoulder. Like it was my fault how much food cost.

"Sorry, Angel. Potatoes, rice, oatmeal. Eggs."

"I don't eat eggs," Angel snapped.

"Fine. Beans are cheap protein, too."

Angel turned back to stare at me. "What are you, fifty?"

I hung my head. "I know."

We trudged on. Sweat plastered my hair to the back of my neck, darkened my T-shirt, stung my eyes. Finally, after what seemed like hours, Angel stopped and pointed.

Civilization. A post office, a nail place, and a little gift shop together in a cluster, and just beyond that . . . Stop & Shop.

"Food!" Angel started to trot. She turned back when I didn't follow. "Come on!"

A gray car was idling at the entrance to the post office. It was plain as a stone, but I couldn't tear my eyes from it. Its directional blinked steadily, like a red beating heart. It made me think of Louise, of her heart that had stopped beating, but that wasn't what upset me.

"Come *on*. We're almost there," Angel called.

"That car."

"What about it?"

"It's waiting for us."

"You're paranoid."

But just then, the woman driver ducked into her rear-view to wave at us.

"Oh, crap, oh, crap," Angel muttered.

I watched, frozen, as the woman signaled a van to pass around her and then began to back up slowly.

It was Ms. Richardson. She bobbed her head to smile at us. "Hi, girls. Stella, I was just thinking about you. I got a couple of novels in I think you're going to love. I'll put them aside for September. How's your summer going?"

"Fine," we said at once. Angel straightened up, but I just kept grinning into the car like an idiot. "Fine. Fine. It's fine," I kept on, kicking into nervous blabber mode.

"So, are you going far? Can I give you a ride?" the librarian asked.

"No thanks, we're all set." Angel patted the car's fender and backed away.

But I absolutely could not help myself. "We're just going in there, into that gift shop. The Salty Cod. Going to get a present for my great-aunt—she loves the stuff in there. That's why we're walking, so she won't know about it. It's a surprise present!" I could feel Angel's eyes burning holes in me, but could I stop? No. "We're doing great, having a great summer, everything's great."

"You live down near Mill River Beach, right?"

"Yep, that's where we live." I chirped it. I heard it as if I was standing next to myself, horrified—a chirp. "With my great-aunt. We're getting her a present!"

"That's a long way in this heat," Ms. Richardson said. "Tell you what. I'm just running into the post office. You girls get your gift and then I'll give you a ride back."

"No, that's okay," Angel started.

"Great!" my blabber self practically yelled. "That'd be *great*, thanks!"

The librarian smiled and pulled in to park. I could feel Angel steaming beside me.

"We can see the Stop & Shop," she hissed. "We were that close."

"I'm sorry."

"I can actually read the signs in the window. Corn, six ears for a buck ninety-nine. Corn would have been good."

"I couldn't help it. I got nervous. I'm *sorry*."

Angel threw her hands around, as if she were clutching for the words to adequately describe what a jerk I was. Finally she shook her head and stormed off to the gift shop. I followed her up and down the aisles, miserable.

There was food there, at least. Among the painted-shell ashtrays, lighthouse sweatshirts, and rubber lobsters, Angel picked up two boxes of saltwater taffy and slammed them on the counter.

* * *

It's really, really awful to be hungry.

Out in the garden, the plants seemed to tease me with their not-ready-to-eat food. At the beach, people unwrapped granola bars and shook out Cheez-Its and popped grapes and guzzled lemonade all around me. As I passed by them, I knew I was eyeing their picnics exactly like a hungry gull, but I couldn't turn away. In my books, every scene involved a meal. Back at the house, every magazine was suddenly full of recipes, and the television shows became nothing more than ads for restaurants and junk food, with scenes of people eating in between. The evenings were the worst, when the families drifted out of the cottages, the mothers doling out snacks and the fathers sizzling burgers on the grills. The smell of meat drove me out of my mind.

I thought back to the report the Family Services lady had read in court, about how my mother had left me without food. It wasn't true. There were boxes of spaghetti and jars of sauce, and a bag of apples. I would have been so happy with that much food now.

The low point came on Thursday night. Earlier, I'd watched the twin boys eating slices of watermelon and then pelting each other with the rinds. After all the renters were safely inside, I'd taken a casual stroll over the lawn. I knelt down when I came upon a rind, pretending to pick something off my sandal. I found three of them. They were covered in sand and ants, but I picked them up. Inside I washed them off and split them with Angel, eating them down to the hard green skin.

"Tomorrow," I said. "Tomorrow we walk to the store again. I won't wreck it."

But Friday it poured all day.

By noon, Angel and I were ready to eat our shoes. I splashed out to the garden and picked off a handful of half-grown string beans, then hunted through the cupboard again, just in case we'd missed something. We had. When I pulled out the jug of maple syrup, thinking that maybe Angel would eat the string beans if they were sweet, I found half a package of stale croutons. I poured hot water over them and stirred them up with the maple syrup. Angel came in and I handed her a bowl. "It's like oatmeal," I said, and pushed some string beans toward her. Angel ate everything without a word. And that was the saddest thing of all.

CHAPTER
◇ 15 ◇

Saturday morning I actually woke up to the sound of my stomach growling. I started to get up, but I fell back from dizziness. I rolled over and got to my feet carefully and dressed.

Voices floated from the cottages—the families were up early packing, getting ready to leave. Angel came downstairs and looked at me hopefully. I shook my head. We sat down to wait, tortured by the smell of bacon and toast.

At nine thirty, we settled ourselves beside the LINGER LONGER sign. The families were all outside stuffing their cars and lashing down bikes and clicking kids into boosters and car seats. One by one, a parent from each cottage came over to return their keys. I had worried that someone would ask to see Louise, but everybody seemed pretty frazzled. They said, "Sorry not to meet her," "Maybe we'll be back next year," and "Hope she's getting around better soon."

Two cars pulled out, waving, and then the woman from the last family came over, holding a badminton racquet. "I'm sorry," she said. "My boys seem to have . . . restrung it."

"That's okay, it happens all the time here," I said. "Kids on vacation, you know."

She pressed a twenty-dollar bill into my hand. "Well, this is to replace it," she said. Then she fished a card from her pocketbook. "My friend's a physical therapist in Boston. Fabulous, a genius with backs." Then she recited a list of things that could go wrong after an injury, which was a lot. I agreed that Louise certainly didn't need any spinal alignment troubles after all this and promised to give her the card.

Then the woman sprang away to chase after one of her twins who had escaped, wrestled him back into the car, and they took off, too.

I turned to Angel. "Want to each take a cottage, or—"

"Do them together," Angel chose in a flash, with panic in her eyes. "I don't remember any of what he said."

I went inside to get the phone—since my mom hadn't called for the past two Saturdays, she'd surely call today. It got reception as far as the picnic table, so that's where I left it.

Then Angel and I opened up Tern. In the kitchen, I opened the refrigerator out of habit. "Angel!" I cried. "Come here. Now!"

Angel came skidding in. "*Ô Jesus querido!*" she whispered prayerfully, gaping at the open refrigerator like she was witnessing a miracle.

We tore into that food like wild dogs at a dump. We ate the two hot dogs cold in three gulps, shook clumps of fried clams into our mouths straight from the containers, and scooped up spoonfuls of cream cheese. I opened the cupboards and found more treasure: a bagel, half a box of spaghetti, a handful of pretzels, some cereal that had gotten stale in the sea air. The freezer held three Popsicles, a couple of fish sticks, and a can of limeade.

Angel and I ate until we didn't want any more. In less than two weeks, I had forgotten what it felt like to have enough to eat. The warm spreading feeling of fullness.

Finally, we packed the rest of the food into a bag. We thought of it at the same time and ran to Gull.

There wasn't a lot of anything: a single sad slice of bologna curling brown at the rim, three of cheese, a half-finished container of strawberry yogurt, a wedge of cantaloupe, a bag with broken cookie pieces in the bottom, and three hamburger rolls. But taken together they'd seem like a feast tomorrow.

Apparently Mr. and Mrs. Sandpiper had decided not to cook on their vacation—their cupboards were empty, but the refrigerator held restaurant leftovers: a piece of pizza, half a shrimp salad sandwich, an egg roll, and a full carton of pad Thai. "*Ô Jesus querido*, we're saved," Angel said, filling a bag.

It was in Sandpiper that we found the first tip. A twenty-dollar bill under the salt shaker, folded into a scribbled thank-you note. We checked the other cottages. Tern produced another twenty, on the bureau between the twin beds. Gull had a ten on the coffee table.

"Cheapskates," Angel muttered. But she was smiling. Fifty dollars—seventy with the racquet money. We brought the money and the food back to our house, along with a suit jacket Mr. Gull had left and a pair of swim fins from Sandpiper, and stashed it. And then we went back over to Tern and got to work.

It was a good thing there were only three cottages to clean that first time. Angel stood in the doorway and threw up her hands, so it was clear I would have to give her directions. First off, I sent her to strip the beds. She did that, but when I came in, all the sheets were lying on the floor in a heap.

"Now you take them to our house," I prodded her. "And you come back with the extra sets that are in the closet where we put them last week."

Angel did that. But again, I had to tell her the next step. "Now we make the beds."

She was just as hopeless at the cleaning. I handed her a broom and told her to straighten up the living room and sweep while I got started in the kitchen. I washed the dishes, shook the crumbs from the toaster, hung up fresh dish towels, tied up the trash. I was about to start on the counters when I noticed Angel was still in the living room.

Nothing looked different.

"What have you been doing?" I asked.

Angel looked insulted.

"You didn't even sweep."

"I swept," Angel said.

I looked down at the floor. There were broom marks in the sand and dust. "You pushed the dirt around, that's all. The point was to get it out of here."

"Well, you should have told me that," Angel huffed.

At first I thought she was just being Angel. But then I thought about it—her mother had died when she was a baby and her father when she was seven. She'd been in six different homes since then. I guess there was a lot of stuff she could have missed.

I gave her a quick lesson in basic sweeping and dustpan techniques, and Angel frowned, but she listened. "Also," I said, "see how everything is jumbled up here on the coffee table? If you pile the puzzles neatly, biggest on the bottom, and put the deck of cards on top, stack the coasters, and put the magazines back on the shelf, it just looks neater. And anything that wasn't here last week—the gum wrapper, the slipper shells, the hair elastic—goes. Okay?"

"Okay," Angel said, her fists balled at her side.

I should have paid more attention to that—her balled-up fists. Instead, I made up a bucket of cleaning solution and laid a sponge beside it. "Go over to Plover, see how we left it last week. Study the counters. Memorize them. Then come back here and get rid of everything you didn't see over there. Put it away or throw it away. Then wash everything—the counters, the cabinets, the refrigerator, the stove, everything. Okay?"

I left Angel and marched into the bathroom and looked around at the mess. The first thing I noticed was a problem with the shower curtain liner. I went over to our house for a quick consultation with Heloise, then grabbed a pair of scissors and came back to Tern.

Angel came in as I was finishing. Her hair and T-shirt

were sopping, and there were streaks of soap down her face. "Nothing's getting cleaner!" she wailed. Then she noticed what I was doing. "You're cutting the shower curtain."

"Just the bottom three inches," I explained. "See how it was getting mold spots? That's from sitting with water on it. You cut off the bottom with pinking shears so it makes a zigzag edge and the water drips off—see, it's easy!"

Something came over Angel then, like a tornado, springing from nowhere but her dark heart, I guess.

"No!" she yelled. "It's not easy! *This* is easy!" She grabbed the liner and jerked it down, hard. Three rings tore off, and she yanked it again and again, until it lay crumpled in the shower stall. "None of this is easy, Stella! Also, I don't give a crap about it! You act like you're so great because you can clean stuff—big deal! Cleaning isn't magic, you know. It isn't holy."

She stormed out. I stood beside the shower, shaking.

Another thing about icebergs, I reminded myself: When you see one, you're only seeing a tiny part of it. Most of it hangs deep under the water, cold and quiet and hard, like a fist around its secret heart.

There was tape back at the house, but no way was I going to walk past Angel to get it. Instead, I found some Band-Aids in the medicine cabinet. One by one, I repaired the ripped holes. *Be the iceberg.* As I was finishing, I heard

Angel's voice from the kitchen.

"I found some jelly in the cupboard," she called.

I pressed my lips together and peeled open another Band-Aid. I was down to the tiny ones now, the ones for little paper cuts.

"I'm eating it right out of the jar."

I did not care. I was an iceberg.

"With my *fingers*! You should come out and save me from myself."

I stood and began to hang the liner back up. Angel came in. She held out a spoon and the jar of jelly. "I'm sorry, Stella. It's just . . . it's just all so hard."

I ignored her some more.

"I'll go make the beds," she sighed. "I know how to do that now."

I shut the door behind her. And then I got to work.

I happen to be very good at cleaning. Not everyone is. Oh, sure, everyone can do a basic job—it's not climbing Mount Everest, or performing brain surgery. But to be really good at it, you have to develop an eye—that's what I call it, anyway, after an art teacher once explained about being an artist. I have developed an eye. That means right away I can see what needs to be done. I can look at a wreck of a countertop and see instantly what's trash, what needs to be put back in its place, what needs to be wiped, and what just needs straightening.

I scoured that bathroom from top to bottom—because that's how you clean a room, from top to bottom. And the cleaning calmed me down and made me see things clearer, the way it always did.

What I figured out was that Angel was wrong the way I was right-handed and tall—she just was, and there wasn't anything anyone could do about it. So there was no point in explaining that cleaning did solve a lot of things. Why, a little thing like lining up the detergent bottle and the spray cleaner on the kitchen sink could settle you down when you were jittery. That's almost magic. My mother was fine—really almost fine—as long as my grandmother was there, keeping things in order. And if that isn't holy, I don't know what is.

I looked around at the little bathroom, which was gleaming now. The summer-day-at-the-beach, full of broken-things-tell-a-story shells, bathroom.

There was a new broken thing in it now: the shower curtain. I wondered what story George would make up about it. I hoped it would be something better than the truth.

"Angel," I called. "Let's go do Gull now. You can just watch this time."

CHAPTER
◇ 16 ◇

Cleaning those cottages took all the tricks I knew, and then I had to invent some new ones. But at two forty-five, sweating and exhausted, we closed the door on the last one.

At the top of the driveway, a station wagon waited patiently, loaded down with vacation stuff. I hadn't noticed it coming in, and I wasn't going to notice it now, either. "Three o'clock means three o'clock," I said. "George said no early birds." Angel tapped her wrist at the car, and I pocketed the key and headed to the picnic table for the phone. Which wasn't blinking. We headed into our house for the master list.

As we passed the roses at the doorway, I had an inspiration. I filled four canning jars with water, then snipped some flowers and made bouquets for the cottages. Then we brought them out to our posts under the LINGER LONGER sign. Immediately, the car that had been waiting pulled in. We gave it a big, smiling wave of welcome.

"Here we go again," I said.

Angel and I told our story about Louise breaking her ankle, and once again no one seemed upset or suspicious. They only wanted to know where the beach was and were there sharks and where was the best place for fried clams.

The second group of renters was different from the first the way families are different, of course—one had two moms, one was from Canada, and one needed a cot for a cousin who'd come along at the last minute—but they were the same, too. In fact, I thought maybe not too much had changed since George's parents had opened the place: Linger Longer was a place for families with little kids, taking vacations in their big cars, and probably the cars had changed more than anything else.

But that second group of renters was different because it brought us Katie. It brought us two Katies, actually. One was a quiet seven-year-old in Tern, and one—my Katie— was about four years old and the opposite of quiet.

Katie Sandpiper latched on to me from the minute she spilled out of the car. She ran right over and grabbed my hand and made me admire her hairdo—a wispy ponytail of hair as pale as corn silk on the top of her head. "Fountain-head," she informed me.

I looked at it from all angles and nodded. "I get it."

She skipped along beside her mother as I opened up Sandpiper for them. Katie pointed to the flowers I carried. "They go over there, on the table." I put them down, and then Katie dragged me around, showing me everything as if it was her home and I was the visitor. "That's the couch," she informed me. "There's the fidgerator."

A boy of about nine walked through then. He was reading a book, and he never looked up, just headed straight into a bedroom.

"Daniel, come back here," his mother called, and I got the feeling she had to call him back a lot. "Say hello and help your father unload the car."

Daniel walked back through again, his nose still in his book. He lifted two fingers an inch off the page as he passed me. "'Lo."

As I was heading out to open Plover for the next family, Mrs. Sandpiper asked, "Now, could you recommend a babysitter?"

My first thought was how dangerous it could be to have

girls from town come here. They might know us, they might ask questions. My next thought was a lot smarter: Babysitters get to eat.

"Actually," I said, "you're looking at one."

As soon as we got everyone settled, I lettered four index-card signs. LINGER LONGER BABYSITTING SERVICE—MATURE, DEPENDABLE, AND YOU DON'T HAVE TO DRIVE US HOME! I added the phone number, then delivered them.

Angel went to the calendar. "We're full from now on. Say thirty or forty bucks each week for cleaning, and maybe another twenty or thirty in babysitting. . . ."

I realized Angel was figuring on splitting the money with me. I opened my mouth to tell her I didn't want any of it, but then I saw what she was doing—tapping her fingers down the weeks, calculating when she could leave—and I closed it.

"Hey, what's this?" she said.

I followed her finger.

Dr. P, cleaning, 9:30. This Monday. The Monday *in two days*. We'd forgotten to look at Louise's calendar! How could we have forgotten to look at Louise's calendar?

"Oh, crap, oh, crap," Angel chanted. "What are we going to do?"

And then I recognized it. "It's okay," I said. "Dr. Payne,

that's her dentist. I remember thinking when she mentioned him one time that 'Pain' was a terrible name for a dentist—he should change it or get a different career. She told me how it was spelled."

I found the number in the phone book. "It's the weekend. There won't be anyone there." Before I could chicken out, I left a message that Louise wanted to reschedule for sometime in August. "Crisis averted," I said, crossing off the appointment.

And then my eye traveled down the calendar. "Angel," I said. "What's this?"

Two weeks away, on a Friday afternoon, was penciled in *Lorraine M., 1 p.m.*

"No clue," Angel said. "A friend? Lunch?"

Lorraine M. Somehow, I felt I knew that name, or I should. "That has to be it—lunch. It won't matter. Louise will be a no-show, and then this Lorraine person will call and we'll make up some excuse," I said. It sounded right, what I'd just said. It made sense.

The next day, Sunday, went pretty much the way the last Sunday had gone—millions of questions in the morning, but by noon, everyone was gone. Like I had last Sunday, I headed for the beach with a book after I'd worked in the garden for a while. I didn't stay too long, because I'd forgotten sunscreen.

When I reached our backyard, I stopped short. Music was coming from upstairs—swelling and beautiful, like violins, but it was a single voice. I rinsed my feet with the garden hose—sand tracked on a wood floor can ruin it—and listened for a while. The words were in another language, but they made my throat ache—"throat tears," I had called the feeling when I was little—so I knew the woman was singing about something very sad. I also knew that Angel's music was a private thing, like her soap opera reports to Louise.

I wandered back to the blueberry bushes. They looked worse than ever—the berries were a little shriveled, and some had even turned black. The leaves were ragged and the bushes themselves looked tired, like they wanted to give up. I suddenly understood they were dying. Maybe nothing I could do for them would be enough, because I wasn't Louise.

Just then, George pulled into the driveway next door. Treb danced beside him while he pulled the mower out of the truck bed. I waved, and he and Treb started over.

"How's everything going?" he asked. "The cottages?"

"Great," I said. "Everybody's out now."

George nodded. "Beach day. Late tide today, so I figured it would be a good time to mow. I haven't heard from

Louise—how's she doing?"

"She's . . . oh, she's the same."

"Well, I'll come in to see her when I'm done. Better get to it."

"George, wait," I said. "Do you know anything about blueberry bushes? These don't look so hot."

George bent and splayed some leaves through his fingers, turning them over a few times. He straightened up. "You can probably kiss 'em good-bye this year. Gypsy moths are eating the leaves." He swept his pipe over the pines and oak scrub. "Pests. Bad year."

"Gypsy moths?"

"The caterpillars, actually. Most years, they're just a nuisance. Every once in a while, though, they're a plague. So many they strip the trees, kill off whole areas. They like oaks best, but in a bad year like this, you're wearing a green T-shirt, you don't want to stand still too long."

"Caterpillars?" I pulled the branches apart and poked through the ragged leaves. "I don't see any."

"They hide in the daytime—can't take the sun." He toed aside some mulch at the base of the bush and crouched beside me. "There. See 'em? Ugly things."

They were ugly—greenish brown and hairy, squirming away from the light. I edged away.

George stood up and rubbed his back. "They come out

at night, climb up the trees, and start eating. Look how bare the oaks are getting. Don't tell me you haven't heard them? God-awful sound . . . the chewing and the droppings spattering down all night long."

"And they're eating my blueberry bushes too? I mean Louise's?" Relief washed through me—those plants weren't grieving to death, and it wasn't my fault. "That's what's wrong?"

"'Fraid so. Well, that grass isn't going to mow itself, you know." George started to leave, but the second piece of his good news finally hit me.

"Wait a minute. Did you just say you can hear them chewing all night?"

"Yep. Disgusting sound, gets in your ears, hard to shake out. Makes you think you're losing your mind. You haven't heard that?"

It was all I could do not to tackle George, I was so happy. Instead I hugged my elbows, hard. "I have! That's great! That's so great! Thank you, thank you, thank you!"

"I'll be darned!" he muttered.

I laughed and squeezed myself harder against the sudden tidal wave of relief. "Right!" I agreed. "I'll be darned!" Tonight, when I heard that awful chewing sound, I would just smile and close my eyes and fall asleep.

Then I stopped short. "Can I stop them?"

"One girl, stop a plague?" George shook his head. "I guess not. But . . . well, you can keep 'em off an individual tree . . . is that what you mean? I've got a couple of apple trees I never let them have. My wife planted them the year before she got sick."

"How do you . . . Wait, oh. You have a wife?"

"Had. She passed."

"Oh. Oh, I'm sorry." I tried to picture George with a wife, and I found it was easy. "Do you have any kids?"

"Wanted to." George looked so forlorn for a minute that I could have kicked myself for bringing it up. But then he gave a little shrug. "I got a crew, though. They're like a family. And speaking of them, we're going fishing tonight on the late tide, which means I'd better get mowing."

I followed George back to his truck. He wheeled the mower onto the lawn and pulled the starter cord. The engine sputtered a second, then died. He tried again and again, with no luck. "Piece of junk." Then he kicked the wheel and cursed.

"Hey," I said, "remember about broken things. Sometimes they have a story to tell you." I suddenly wanted George to know that I understood that now. That we had that in common. A tie.

George kicked the tire again. "And sometimes they're just plain broken." He looked up then, too fast for me to hide my disappointment.

He smiled at me. "And sometimes, Stella by Starlight, they're just out of gas!"

He went to the shed and came back with a red tank. I held the funnel while he filled the mower's belly.

We listened to the gasoline chugging in, and I took a deep breath—I always liked the smell of gasoline. It smells clean and exciting, like you're about to go someplace new.

George sniffed, too. "I love that smell. That's the smell of a finest-kind day."

I knew he wanted me to ask what a finest-kind day was, so I did.

"It's a fishing thing," he said. "Finest kind means the best. Best quality, just perfect. Some days you set out and you don't know where you'll end up. But your boat is seaworthy, the wind is calm, and the sea is full of hungry fish. And you've got a full tank of gas."

"Finest kind," I said, handing him the mower cap. Then I remembered. "Hey, George. Your apple trees? How did you protect them?"

"Wrap the trunks in burlap. The caterpillars hide there when the sun comes out. I shake the burlap out and kill 'em."

I looked back to where the squirming mass of caterpillars was and tried to imagine squashing them. "What else?" I asked.

"What else? Nothing. They die, your tree lives."

"No. I mean what else could I do? I don't want to kill them."

George capped the tank and wiped his hands before he straightened to look at me. "Louise's blueberry bushes? You're going to try to save them for her?"

I nodded.

"Well, some folks tie greased rags around the trunks. The caterpillars can't climb past 'em. Seems like a lot of work, but . . . I got some extra rags at my place. I could bring around some motor grease."

I thought for a minute. Rags and grease. "That's okay, George." I gave Treb an ear scratch that made him look the way I felt. "Louise has everything I need."

It took a long time, because there were so many bushes and they each had a bunch of stems. When I finished, I was sweaty and dirty and greasy and scratched all over, but happy. I stood at the sink, washing up and letting the happiness flood through me like cool water, filling every thirsty cell.

I heard the mower go silent. And I remembered. "Angel! George's coming over. He wants to see Louise!"

Angel trotted down the stairs, smiling. "I know. I saw him pull in. I got it covered." She pointed to a huge vase of roses on the coffee table in the living room. "They're from her boyfriend." Then she pointed to a suit jacket hanging over a kitchen chair. "The one whose jacket is here."

"What a coincidence," I said. "It looks just like the one Mr. Gull left." I recognized the roses, too. "Louise's boyfriend picked roses from her garden? That's so lame of him."

"George will be too brokenhearted to think of that. Love hurts, but it's for his own good."

I nodded out the window. "Well, here he comes."

George stopped at the kitchen door to shake the grass clippings off his clothes and make Treb lie on the step before he came in. One more thing I liked about him—he was thoughtful about Louise's clean kitchen.

"You got something dead in your garden," he said.

CHAPTER
❖ 17 ❖

" I caught Treb digging like crazy earlier. Right where those pumpkins are. I figure you got something dead in your fertilizer. Probably fish meal. Sorry. Don't think he did any damage, though. I smoothed it all back. Although . . ."

I forced myself to breathe naturally. In and out. Through my nose. Louise was deep, really deep.

"Although a funny thing—I didn't see any sign of those pumpkins of yours. It's been two weeks. They ought to have sprouted by now. . . ."

"Huh," I said, and my voice was only a little squeaky. "*That's* weird."

"Well, thanks for telling us," Angel said. She took a step toward the door, but George wasn't going anywhere.

"Where's Louise?" he asked.

"She's out," Angel answered.

George looked puzzled. "Her car's here."

"Her boyfriend picked her up," Angel said, practically yawning with how bored she was trying to sound. As if Louise went out with boyfriends every day.

George didn't even try to hide his surprise. "Her *boyfriend?*"

"Yep, her new boyfriend. They're on a date. The one who sent her those roses over there. He left his jacket."

I busied myself washing some dishes because I couldn't even look at Angel.

"Louise has a boyfriend? Since when?"

"Since a long time ago, actually. He's actually her old boyfriend. But he went out on a spy mission years ago, and he got caught and everyone thought he was dead. And then he got amnesia, which is why he forgot about her all these years. Do you want to look at his jacket?"

"Look at his . . . ? Ah . . . no. No thanks. I'll be off. Those fish aren't going to catch themselves, you know."

Later that night, I sat down with a notebook and a pen, doing something I never thought I'd get to do until I was an adult. Angel walked into the kitchen just as I was finishing, and my pride took over my good sense. "My first one," I said, holding up my notebook.

"First what?" Angel asked, pretending to be bored.

"My first hint. I'm sending a hint to Heloise. And the best part is that it's for one of her favorite subjects—old panty hose! Hints about onion bags are actually the most popular. Old panty hose are second, though—I've got about a dozen hints about those."

"Old panty hose? Who do you know who even has old panty hose?" Angel glanced up toward Louise's room. "Oh, right."

"Right," I said. And I guess I was just kind of crazy with relief and happiness from my afternoon, because there's no other explanation for what I did next: I handed her my notebook. "What do you think?"

Angel read aloud, *"Dear Heloise, I love your column. I think if more people took your advice, the world would be a better place. I am very proud to be able to tell you a new use for those old panty hose after they get runs in them. You can tie pieces of them around blueberry bush stems (or other trees or bushes!) and slather them with Crisco so gypsy moth caterpillars won't climb up and eat all the leaves! Sincerely, your friend, Stella. P.S. Please feel free to use my real name."*

I looked up at Angel, and too late I saw my mistake—she was thinking up something smart to say to ruin my letter. But then her expression changed.

"That's a good one," she said, all sweet. "I'm going to write her a letter, too."

"You can't just write her a letter," I explained. "Heloise is very busy. She gets hundreds of letters a week, and she has to test out all those hints. Of course she has a whole bunch of people to help her now. Still, she can't take time to just say 'Hi, how are you?' kind of stuff. You can only write if you have a really good hint." Like mine. Which Heloise was going to love.

"Oh, I have a really good hint all right," she said. She took my pen and ripped a fresh page out of my notebook. When she sat down at the table, I stood behind her because I couldn't help it—I wanted to know what her hint was.

Dear Heloise, she wrote. *I have a really good hint for what to do with those old panty hose after they get runs in them.*

"You can't just copy mine," I warned her.

"Don't worry. This is definitely my own idea." She gave me another big smile—this time so fake she might as well have been wearing wax teeth. I read what she wrote anyway: *The best part of my hint is that it will work for onion bags, too: THROW THEM AWAY!!!*

I tore up her letter and threw it at her, which just made her laugh.

CHAPTER
◦ 18 ◦

I went outside to put my letter in the mailbox, and then I walked around back and lay down on the picnic table. What made me maddest was that she was ridiculing Heloise—Heloise, who never did anything but good in the world, who made millions of people's lives better. I went over some of my favorite tips I'd learned from her, and after a while, I calmed down.

There was no moon, but a couple of the cottages had yellow lights on in the bedrooms. Fireflies drifted up like embers from an imaginary campfire, and the air was soft and sweet with honeysuckle. It was a pretty night. The phrase reminded me of what George had said that first time we'd met him—that it was a pretty day. I wondered if he was on his boat now, with his crew. I wondered if he slept at sea sometimes, if his sleep "fingerprint" had to do with the waves.

"Shove over."

I shimmied over to the edge of the table. Angel arranged herself on the other edge. Not touching. The crickets stopped chirping, as if they were waiting to see what would happen next. After a while, her flip-flop brushed my sneaker. I shifted my foot away.

She tapped it again, harder. "About tonight," she said.

I wasn't in the mood to talk about it, but a small "hmmm" slipped out.

"I'm sorry. But you're kind of obsessed with this Heloise person."

"I know I am," I said after a while.

"So what is it with her, anyway?"

I clasped my hands under my head and sighed. I still didn't want to talk about it, but I was suddenly too tired not to. Being an iceberg takes a lot of effort. "When my grandmother died, we had to clean out her stuff. My mother said I could keep one thing, and she'd have to yard-sale the rest. I picked her Hints from Heloise clippings."

"How come?"

"Because you could count on things at my grand-mother's. Everything was always where it belonged. You could go blind at my grandmother's house and you'd do fine—you'd never trip over a pile of laundry or crash into a chair that had been tossed into the hall. By the time we had to clean out my grandmother's, I'd been living with my mother in this little apartment for a couple of months, and well, it was really different."

I stopped. It suddenly hurt to draw a breath. I had missed my grandmother so much when we were cleaning out her stuff. I had missed her Hints-from-Heloise home. I had been so scared by how my mother had paced and paced in that little apartment.

I breathed in, taking careful little sips. "Anyway. I figured maybe those clippings held some secrets to how things were at my grandmother's, so I should pick them. Since then, I've been collecting them myself, mostly from magazines I find lying around, in recycling and stuff. A couple of times I ripped them out of magazines in waiting rooms—I don't think that's stealing, do you? Well, I guess maybe it is."

"Nah," Angel said. "I don't think you should worry about that."

I tipped my head back. Even upside down, Louise's house looked just right. "You know, if Louise had had grandchildren, I bet they would have loved visiting here. I wish I'd told her I appreciated things like how she always made chili on Sundays, or always had cupcake liners in the baking cupboard or stamps and envelopes in the drawer. She was always prepared."

"I guess," Angel said. She was quiet for a long minute after that. "I'm sorry for messing with you about that letter," she said at last.

"That's okay. I don't have much of a sense of humor these days. Too hungry."

Angel snaked her hand into her pocket and pulled out two Dum Dums. "I had the brilliant idea of checking my winter jacket yesterday." She handed me one. "Truce?"

We lay there for a while, considering the sky and how delicious a stale Dum Dum could taste. And then I heard it. "Listen to that, Angel. That raining sound. It's gypsy moth caterpillars. George told me. I really wish we didn't have to lie to him, by the way. About Louise having a boyfriend, I mean. Anyway, he said these caterpillars chew all night and their droppings rain down. It's called frass." I rolled over to face her. "Why didn't you admit you heard it when I asked you?"

Angel cocked her head, listening. "I've never heard that before."

"Come on. When you lie in bed and everything else is

quiet, you have to be able to hear it. Why wouldn't you tell me?"

Angel shrugged. "I don't hear anything at night. I sleep with my earphones on."

"Oh." I finished the lollipop, making sure I had extracted every molecule of candy from the stick. It occurred to me that since I'd just spilled so much to Angel, maybe I could get away with asking a question. "What's with the music all the time, anyway?"

"It's not just music," Angel said. "It's fado. Portuguese songs about fate. You wouldn't understand."

"So explain it."

"You can't explain fado, you have to feel it. It's about *saudade*, and there's no English for it. The closest might be 'the ache of missing someone,' but that's not it."

"So it's songs about missing people?"

"It can be. It's about how hard life is. About how dangerous the sea is, how much love hurts, about being poor. Sad stuff like that. Actually, mournful is a better word." Angel levered herself up on her elbows. "In fact, that's how you know if your fado performance was successful—if your audience is crying."

"So why do you listen to it?"

"My mother was a *fadista*. She used to perform at a club in New Bedford. The CD was hers. She listened to it, and now I listen to it."

And then I put it together. "So that's what I heard that afternoon. Huh . . . fado."

Angel shook her head. "I don't have speakers. You must have heard something else, maybe a radio from the cottages."

"No. It was coming from upstairs, from your side, I'm sure."

Angel's face closed. She rolled off the picnic table and went inside.

Angel was wrong. I did understand about *saudade*. I knew the ache of missing someone. The only thing was, sometimes I didn't know who that person was.

Suddenly, I felt a prickle on my ankle. I brushed at it, but the bristly thing stuck. I stifled a scream and slapped the gypsy moth caterpillar off. Then I marched inside, pulled out Louise's gardening books, and set to work learning about the enemy.

Scientific name: *Lymantria dispar*. Carolus Linnaeus is a hero of mine. He's the one who classified everything— every single living thing. He put it in a family tree and gave it a name that makes sense. That guy was all about orderliness. I bet if he and Heloise had lived at the same time, they would have gotten married. If Heloise and Carl had had a kid, that kid would have been a lot like me. Anyway, the name Linnaeus gave the gypsy moth means "destroyer."

And according to Louise's gardening books, the gypsy moth is one of the worst invasive pests. It was brought to the United States in 1869 by a French scientist living in Massachusetts, who thought if he bred them with silkworms, he'd end up with a tough moth that spun silk. Instant billionairehood, he probably figured. What he ended up with instead was a big mess: It wasn't love at first sight for the two species, and then some of the gypsy moths escaped into the wild. Within a couple of years, they were spreading like crazy, devouring the delicious forests of New England.

Or the caterpillars were. When they first emerge from their eggs, the larvae hang from branches by long silken threads. The wind spreads them, sometimes a mile or more away. The caterpillars grow by molting five or six times, eating constantly at night between the molts, until they turn into moths, sometime in July.

I put the book down and rolled over and scratched where the caterpillar had been stuck. My skin crawled all night.

CHAPTER

· 19 ·

Monday evening, I took the first babysitting job. It was for Katie Sandpiper, while the rest of the family went out for a baseball game. "Katie's a little too *fragile* for crowds tonight. We've been having a meltdown here," Katie's mother told me on the phone.

When I walked in, Katie's face was red and furious.

"She got gum in her hair," Mrs. Sandpiper explained. "I've been trying to cut it out, but she won't let me get near her. Maybe you could try when she's . . ." Mrs. Sandpiper tipped her head onto her folded hands and closed her eyes.

"I'm not going to sleep!" Katie warned her fiercely. "Not ever!"

One look at Katie's face and you could almost believe that.

As soon as the car had pulled away, I checked the cupboard. "Katie, how about if we put some peanut butter in your hair?" I asked.

"Okay!" she agreed, as if she was astounded at what a good idea I'd had. "And jelly in yours!"

"No, this one's just for you. Come on with me." I handed Katie the jar of Jif and walked her over to our house. Angel was at the kitchen table, hunched over a catalog.

"This is Katie. Watch her for a second." I plunked Katie on the counter, then went up to my room and read over the hint that I had remembered.

I came back and spooned out a clump of peanut butter and completely wrapped the gum snarl with it. Angel put her catalog down to watch, but she didn't comment.

"Where's your mommy?" Katie asked as I began to work it in.

"She's not here. Bend your head down."

"She's in the garden," Angel offered. "She's *always* in the garden."

I shot Angel a look, and she raised her eyebrows,

innocent. "Well, she is. In fact, Katie, we can't get her *out* of the garden."

"Oh." Katie leaned up to my ear. "Is that your sister?" she asked in a loud whisper.

"That's my . . . um . . . friend. That's Angel."

While Katie and Angel eyed each other, I worked the peanut butter in. Gradually, the gum wad broke up into oily balls, just as Heloise had promised. I began tugging the pieces out.

"So where's your kids?" Katie asked me.

"Katie, I'm eleven. Angel is twelve. Actually, I'll be twelve, too, next Thursday. We're too young to have kids. Now lean over the sink for the last part."

Katie asked a dozen more questions as I lathered dish soap through her greasy hair, and a dozen more while I washed that out. Back at the cottage, she never stopped chattering while we ate Popsicles and I taught her to play Candy Land. She was still at it when her family got home.

"I beat Stella twice times at Candy Land, and she doesn't have any kids," she told her mother as she paid me. "And her mommy was in the garden tonight."

Mrs. Sandpiper looked up. "How's she doing? Getting around better?"

"Oh, about the same."

And then she noticed. "Hey!" she said, riffling through

Katie's hair in amazement. "Look at you!"

I told her how I'd done it, and she peeled another ten out of her wallet. "Genius bonus."

Tuesday was the Fourth of July. Mrs. Gull came over to ask if we wanted to come to the parade with them. Angel and I exchanged fast looks and shook our heads right away.

"I think we'll just hang around with Louise," Angel said. "Keep her company."

I nodded and slid Angel a smile. That was exactly how I was feeling too. "Do you think about her much?" I asked when everybody had left. "Do you ever wonder where she *is*?"

Angel made a face and yanked her thumb in the direction of the garden. "Just past the zucchini," she said.

"That's just her body. I know where that is. I mean the part of her that was kind of crabby, but kind of looking out for us, too. Like when she made brownies that time, she pretended it was just to use up some eggs before they went bad. You know, the part that was . . . her? Do you ever wonder where that is?"

"Nope," Angel said. "It's out there with the rest of her, I guess. With the worms."

"All right, all right. Change of subject." I went to the window. "It's kind of foggy, but I think I'll go to the beach.

You want to come with me?"

"I don't swim."

"Oh." And then I decided to risk it. "Because of . . . your father?"

"I don't swim," she said again, sharper. "I don't know how." She left the kitchen, and I heard her climb up the stairs to her room.

I followed her and knocked on her closed door. "Look, I could teach you," I offered. "To swim. You want to?"

When Angel didn't answer, I opened the door a little.

She was on her bed, thumbing through a catalog. "No," she said without looking up. She didn't seem mad, but she didn't seem in any mood to be argued with, either. I decided to change the subject again.

I waved my arms over the sea of wrinkled clothes that carpeted the room from wall to wall. "Um . . . time to mow the laundry?"

Angel turned around and pretended to be seeing the problem for the first time. She raised her shoulders in a "Go figure" shrug. "Louise isn't keeping up," she mused.

"Funny," I said. But then I thought about it. Louise always did our laundry. "Puh. I don't like people messing around my machines" was what she said every time I tried to do a load myself. She was so firm about it, I didn't bother telling her I'd been operating washing machines and dryers since I was nine. But maybe Angel hadn't.

"Angel, do you know how to do laundry?"

Angel rolled over and studied the ceiling as she considered the question. "I get the basic concept. But . . . um . . ." She flipped over again and went back to her catalog.

"Look. Bring it down. We have to do all the wash from the cottages anyway."

Angel let out a big dramatic sigh, but she got up. We stripped her bed and rolled her clothes into the sheets. I led Angel down to the cellar and introduced her to the machines and how they worked—Angel looked like she was taking a tour of the NASA rocket launch controls. And all day long, we did laundry—five loads of sheets and towels for the cottages and three whole loads for Angel's things. Afterward, I gave Angel a lesson in folding, and she devoted herself to folding her clothes with so much care, you'd have thought she was making origami cranes. In between all this, we watched television and ate up the rest of the cottage food.

When it was time for Louise's soap, I went upstairs to take a nap—for real, this time. I woke up in a panic. In my dream, I was trying to remember who Lorraine M. was, and it was close, but every time I tried to grab it, it drifted away.

I got up and crossed to my window. The fog had lifted

a little, but everything still looked gray and soft. Below, in the garden, Angel was giving her report.

"He walks in, thinking he's going to have this great reunion with his wife—he's got the flowers and the chocolate, the whole deal. He walks in, all 'Oh, darling, I know it's a shock, but how I've missed you!' stuff. And then he stops. He looks at the table. Two wineglasses. Two. He gets the picture and storms off before she can explain.

"Then for the rest of the show, all anyone talks about is how *confused* they all are. They're all so confused about him appearing out of the blue. They're confused about how they feel about him. They're worried they're going to confuse him. He's worried he's confusing them. They should call it Lame Valley, if you ask me. Oh, I did the laundry today. You have some cool machines."

At the window I couldn't help smiling.

That evening, I sat on the back steps watching the families have their cookouts. The last light of sunset pouring over the scene reminded me of syrup, but that was probably because I was so hungry. The kids ran around with sparklers, and once in a while a firecracker bloomed in the distance with a deep thud.

Angel came out and sat at the far end of the steps. "Happy Independence Day." She blew through her hair.

"We sure are independent."

"We sure are." In front of me were the cottages that were going to need cleaning again on Saturday, and behind me was Louise's house, where there wasn't any food and there was an endless stream of chores to do. I felt like a traitor to my country, but just then, independence didn't seem all it was cracked up to be. Independence seemed like another way of saying nobody cared about you.

"Angel, the other places you lived. Were they that bad? Worse than here?"

Angel leaned over and scratched at a mosquito bite on her shin. "No. Well, one was, but mostly they were okay—they were okay places to live. The people took in foster kids because they wanted to do a good deed, I guess." She paused and rested her head on her knee. "But I wasn't anybody's *destino*, you know?"

She went in and left me alone with my independence again.

CHAPTER
◇ 20 ◇

When I got home from the beach Thursday afternoon, I checked my blueberry bushes, as usual. And for the first time, I could see for sure that they were getting better—the leaves looked less crumpled and there were even a few fresh green ones. The berries looked slightly bigger. I nearly skipped up to the kitchen door, wishing Louise were inside so I could tell her I'd saved them with her panty hose and her Crisco.

Angel was at the open refrigerator. She bent down to check the bins, and her tank top strap slid off her shoulder.

"What are you wearing?" I demanded.

Angel smiled with pride and pulled her strap aside to show me a bra so bright it would scorch your retinas. Black lace over hot pink satin, sparkling with rhinestones.

"You don't need a bra."

"Oh, I needed this bra," Angel assured me. She turned back to the empty refrigerator and groaned. "All I've had to eat today is relish."

"I had Froot Loops dust," I told her. "Where did you get it?"

"Victoria's Secret. Louise gets the catalogs. I guess they have stuff for plus size." Angel rattled the vegetable bins open and slammed them shut again.

"But how?"

Angel snapped her bra strap with a smug grin. "Duh— same way Louise got stuff. Call the number on the back of the catalog, give the lady her credit card number, and the mailman does the rest. Don't look at me like that."

"Like what?"

"That look you always have. Pinched up. Like you're worried something's going to happen." Angel opened and closed the empty cupboard. It sounded hollow.

"I do not always look worried."

"Yeah, you do."

"Well . . . look around, Angel. Things do happen."

"Exactly," said Angel. "Things do happen. That's fate.

Fado. And all your worrying isn't going to change that."

"Angel, you used Louise's credit card! That's not fate, that's . . . well, it's probably a crime. What if someone keeps track of that stuff?"

"Look. Louise was getting money to feed me and buy me clothes. Massachusetts *wants* me to have clothes. Who am I to argue with a whole state?"

I felt there was something wrong with Angel's reasoning, but I couldn't see exactly what it was. That was Angel—I always felt like I was arguing the wrong thing with her. The thing *next to* the thing I was trying to argue about. But it was true that the state had been paying Louise, and that the point of the money was to take care of her—and me, too—which meant clothes and—

It hit me so hard, my mouth actually watered. My conscience argued with my empty stomach. My empty stomach won. "Angel. Once, when my mom went away, she left me her credit card and told me to order pizza. I called. And they delivered."

Angel's face lit up. "Genius!" Second time that week I'd been called that.

"I don't know, though. It's not our card. . . ."

But Angel was already on the phone to Mama's Pizzeria. "Pepperoni," she said, and you could practically hear the drool in her voice.

"With peppers," I mouthed, remembering scurvy.

"Make that two pizzas. One pepperoni and one pepperoni with peppers," she said. "How fast can they come?" She listened for a minute. "Good. And two Cokes."

I held up my fingers.

"Make that four Cokes," she corrected.

I held up my fingers again.

"I mean ten Cokes. And make those pizzas *large*."

Friday night was a big night for the parents to go out to dinner—I guess after a week solid with their kids, they needed a different kind of vacation. Both Angel and I got hired—I took Sandpiper and Angel went over to Gull, where she sat for the other Katie.

My Katie's mother showed me dinner. Organic mac and cheese, carrot sticks, and mango applesauce. Angel and I had eaten leftover pizza for breakfast and lunch, but I was suddenly starving.

"Katie's only eating orange food this week," Mrs. Sandpiper sighed. "There are some tangerines in the fridge. Or just mix ketchup and mustard and give it to her on anything nutritious you can think of. I'm running out of ideas. Daniel's eating with Shawn next door. We'll be back by ten." Then she and Mr. Sandpiper left.

I made dinner right away and ate my plateful of orange

food. Katie ate one bite of everything, then climbed down from her chair.

"You done?" I asked her.

Katie Sandpiper stuck out her tongue. "I hate orange food." I emptied her macaroni onto my plate, every last elbow. Then the carrot sticks. I scraped the pan out onto my plate, too, and scarfed it all down.

"You eat a lot," Katie said.

"Tonight I do. You want anything else?"

"Popsicles. Purple."

We took the Popsicles outside and sat on the steps of the little deck. A sliver of a moon hung just above the trees, shining just enough light to see the Mill River winding through the marsh. "Fireflies!" Katie hollered, and shot off the step, tossing her Popsicle into the bushes. Within minutes, the yard was full of kids. Katie Gull dragged Angel out. She ran off with Katie Sandpiper, and Angel came to sit beside me.

She stuck her stomach out with a proud grin. "Two hamburgers. A giant bag of chips."

"Oh, meat!" I sighed with envy. I patted my own belly. "A whole box of macaroni and cheese. And I might not be done yet."

My Katie came over then, her hands cupped in front of her. "Close your eyes," she ordered. I closed my eyes and felt the tickle of lightning bug feet on my right knee. I opened them and didn't even have to fake my amazement for Katie—that tiny weightless thing, exploring the mountain of my knee so carefully. Katie sat down and watched with me. She leaned her head against my shoulder and was still, and then she leaped up again, as if I were the source of some energy and she had just recharged, and joined the bigger kids in freeze tag.

I bent over the firefly and offered it my finger, which it delicately accepted. At the tip of my nail, it lit up.

CHAPTER
◇ 21 ◇

There were only two cottages to clean that second changeover, because both Sandpiper and Tern were two-week rentals. Like before, we ate whatever we wanted of the food we found and packed up the rest, which wasn't much that time.

I left Angel in Gull with her stack of linens, and I took Plover. An hour and a half later, I locked it up, all clean and ready.

In Gull, I found Angel polishing the toaster. She waved her hands around the cottage with a hopeful look on her face. "Well?"

I looked around. It wasn't great, but it was good enough. I raised my fist, and Angel grinned and bumped it. We tucked the tip money into the Earl Grey tin, made two more babysitting cards and two more bouquets, and then we were ready.

Both of the new families pulled in early, but Angel and I didn't see any reason to make them wait. By two thirty in the afternoon, everybody had unpacked and gone off to the beach or miniature golf or whatever it was tourists did on vacation.

I wandered over to my blueberries, expecting them to look really perked up by now. A couple of the bushes were, but it was as if someone had hit the pause button on most of them. Or maybe even rewind. They were looking crumpled and gray again, like they'd run out of juice.

The panty hose-and-Crisco ties were still in place, but my blueberry bushes were dying again. Most of them, anyway.

SAT: Stop, Access, Think. That's what Heloise recommends doing when you've got a big problem.

I crossed my arms over my head and looked up at the clear blue sky. Access means gather whatever you've got. Okay, year after year, these bushes had produced berries. But this year they were in big trouble. The only thing different about this year was the gypsy moths, so somehow, they were involved. Except I'd stopped them from eating the leaves. The only difference between the healthier-looking bushes and the sick ones was . . . It took me a while to see it. When I did, it didn't seem to make sense: The healthy ones were clustered under the two pine trees—the others were all under oaks.

Think. I turned my gaze from the oaks to the pines, and back again. And again and again. And finally I knew.

I ran inside and up to Louise's closet.

Angel was right: There must have been a hundred dresses in there. Well, thirty or forty at least. I swept armload after armload off their hangers and heaped them on her bed. Then I tied them into a huge flowery bundle and lugged it back outside.

It didn't take nearly as long as the panty hose solution. As I tied the bright clothing to the oak branches, I imagined Louise watching. "I guess you've got the makings of a gardener after all," I imagined her saying. Louise hadn't been much of a smiler, and when she did it, it looked like it hurt her face, but I had her smile in my imagination anyway. It made her face look really pretty.

I draped the last dress over a forked branch and tied off the sleeves, then looked over what I had done. The dresses floated above my blueberry bushes like huge tropical blossoms, drifting a light, fluttery shade over them.

Suddenly I wished that just once I had seen Louise wear a single one of them. It would be nice if all this fluttering could remind me of her, maybe moving around her kitchen in the mornings. A puff of breeze filled the dress beside me; it emptied again with a rustling sigh and I thought, Well, that will do. Louise is breathing out here again.

As I started down the ladder for the final time, I heard George's pickup pull in. When he stepped out, I waved him over.

"Laundry?" he asked.

I shook my head. "Gypsy moths again. The bushes under the oaks were dying because the gypsy moths ate all the oak leaves—look, see how the branches are almost bare? The blueberry bushes were getting more sun than they were used to. They have really shallow roots, so no matter how much I watered them, they were baking. I fixed it. I mean, Louise and I fixed it."

"Good thing," George said. "Lots of folks in town waiting for her pies."

"I know that." I smiled, remembering what Louise had told me on the day she'd died. "She said you'd walk a mile on your knees for a slice."

George raised his hands. "That is the truth. A mile over broken glass. In shorts!" He laughed. Then he looked serious. "Louise must be awfully pleased. Not that she'll show it, a course."

I climbed up a few rungs of the ladder and sat so I was at George's level. "What do you mean?"

"Oh, she's such a Yankee. Never wants to let on what she's feeling. You need a crowbar to pry a compliment out of her. I'll bet she hasn't come out and told you, but she must be awfully happy to have you around."

I suddenly felt a little wobbly, as if I might be about to fall. "I don't know," I said, gripping the ladder rails tighter. "Maybe she's just happy about the money. Did she tell you about that? About how she gets paid to take care of me?" I held my breath.

"You know about that?" George looked over at the house. When he looked back at me, I suddenly wished I hadn't said anything. I didn't want to know.

"And you think that's why she's doing it?"

My shoulders gave a small shrug. Maybe I did.

George shook his head. "Apparently the state pays about six thousand dollars a year for each of you. Louise is saving it for you girls. Said it ought to be a tidy sum by the time you're college age." He looked over at the house and lowered his voice, as if he was afraid Louise could hear him. "Don't you tell her I told you. She'll have my hide."

Just then, the Sandpiper family pulled in. Katie shot

over as soon as her dad sprang her from her car seat. I waved to him that I'd got her, then I scooped her up.

She started in right away with a minute-by-minute report of the family's visit to the fish pier. The report starred her, of course.

I watched George as he listened, and thought how sad it was that he and his wife hadn't had any kids. He looked so peaceful and happy, smiling down at Katie as if there was nothing in the whole world he wanted to do more than listen to her chatter.

Then Katie asked me a question that startled him. "Is your mommy still in the garden?"

"Your mother?" George asked me. "Is she visiting?"

"She means Louise," I explained. I hoisted Katie higher, so she could see over the hedge. "Nope, you can see she's not there right now, kidlet."

The kitchen door opened and Angel hurried over, as if we were having a party she didn't want to miss. The way I was feeling, we kind of were.

"Stella's mommy is always in the garden," Katie told George. "Stella can't get her out of the garden."

"That so?" George turned to me and then to Angel, looking relieved. "You know, for a while, I've been thinking . . . well, I don't know what I've been thinking. But it's good to know she's getting out to the garden again. I'll go in and talk to her. We've got some paperwork to go over."

"Oh, too bad, you just missed her. Off with the boyfriend again." Angel rolled her eyes. Then she leaned in toward him like they were in on a secret. "You know, maybe it would be easier if you stayed away for a while. Just so she doesn't feel . . . *confused*."

George took off his hat and ruffled the hair on the back of his head—he was the one who seemed confused. "Well," he said a couple of times. "Well, they're waiting for me back at the boat. And that grass isn't going to—"

"Mow itself, you know," I chimed in with George. His eyebrows shot up, and then he laughed and shook his head.

Angel walked with George as he headed for his truck. I set Katie on the ground, took her hand, and followed.

"Sure," I heard George say to Angel. "You run a boat, you have to have a survival suit for everyone in your crew. It's regulation."

"Do you keep an extra, though? In case someone extra is on board sometime?"

George looked down at Angel, and I could tell Louise had never told him about Angel's father. "No," he said. "I've got a three-man crew, and there's me, so I've got four suits. I keep a life jacket for Treb here, but that's it. Why?"

"Well, maybe you should get another one. Just in case."

George shrugged. "They're expensive, you know. I can

think of a lot of things I should do with five hundred dollars before getting an extra survival suit. Like a new bilge pump. The crew's down at the dock right now, working on it. I'll bet there's a thousand dollars' worth of repairs coming up." He turned around and pointed back to our house. "Or new gutters. Looks like I'll have to hire someone this fall. It's always something."

They'd reached the pickup. George banged down the tailgate.

"You'd do that for Louise?" Angel asked. "Put new gutters on her house?"

Angel turned to flash me a look—*He's even more in love with her than I'd thought!* I waved Katie off to her mom, who was waiting on Sandpiper's steps, and walked over to the pickup.

"Her house?" George repeated. "Nah, that's my house. Louise lives there in exchange for managing Linger Longer for me. The repair bills are all mine." He pulled the mower out, and it hit the ground with a thud. "You girls take care, now."

CHAPTER
22

"Well?" Angel asked, for the third or fourth or tenth time. She was wedged into her favorite spot on the counter, beside the refrigerator. "What are we going to do? Do we have to leave?"

My chest still hurt as though I had been kicked in the heart, but I lifted my head off the table. "It's all been for nothing. It was never her house." I put my head back down into the cradle of my arms.

Angel picked up the chicken and rooster salt and pepper shakers, made them kiss, then put them down, lining them up together on the same counter tile I always kept them on.

The one Louise had always kept them on. "Okay, then." She didn't move off the counter, though—she just sat there staring at me for a long time.

"All right. Me too," I finally said, knowing what she was thinking. "I wish we could stay, too." For so many reasons. Because of the blueberries. Because my mother had been here. Because we had worked so hard and because I hated quitting things. Because of George, and Katie and all the new families that were coming. Because of Angel. And Louise. "But . . ."

"I know." Angel glanced out the window to where George was mowing. "Are you going to tell him?"

I nodded. I couldn't say the word "yes" out loud.

"Now?"

I nodded again.

Angel nodded, too. "Okay. Back to plan A, then. I'll get my stuff."

"Where are you going?"

"New Bedford. My aunt wrote. She's there now, staying with a friend of a relative of a friend or something. I guess I'll go there. Maybe hide out until she gets a place to live. I don't know." She slid off the counter. "But I'm not going into another home."

Angel pulled the Earl Grey tin off the shelf and counted out the money. "A hundred eighty-six," she said. She counted out ninety-three dollars and laid it on the table in front of me.

I picked up the money and tried to think of a single thing it would buy me. I gave it back to Angel. "Use it to get to your aunt. Don't hitch," I said. "That's a *rule*, got it? And eat some fruit once in a while."

Angel smiled a little, then leaned over and hugged me hard. She stuffed the money into her pocket and turned to leave. "I know I should go out there and tell him with you," she said, pausing at the doorway. "But I can't."

"It's okay."

"I'm sorry."

"It's okay."

And then I went outside.

George was starting on the little strip of grass beside Louise's house. His house, I corrected myself. "I have to tell you something. It's about Louise. It's something bad," I practiced as I walked over. I planted myself in his path, taking tiny sips of air in and out to steady myself.

George leaned down and cut the mower. "Hey."

"I have to tell you something," I said. And my voice was only a little shaky. "It's about Louise." Then I stopped—the new Mr. and Mrs. Gull were heading over from their cottage, swinging their toddler between them.

"Do you happen to have a child safety gate here?"

Mrs. Gull asked. "Please say yes. We each thought the other one packed it, and—"

"I really thought you said you had it," Mr. Gull cut in.

"No, I remember you said you had it, I'm sure—"

Mr. and Mrs. Gull kept breaking into each other's sentences and laughing about how impossible it had been to pack with Trevor being mobile. The little boy tried to make a break for it, but Mr. Gull swept him up under his arm, still squirming. "This little guy is really motoring around these days. He's into everything. . . ."

"Sorry, no," George said. "The nearest shopping center is in Hyannis. But maybe you could try the hardware store here."

Mrs. Gull sighed, and Mr. Gull planted his little boy on his hip. They turned to leave.

"Wait," I said. "There are some adjustable screens in the shed—the old-fashioned kind you slide open to fit the window? Maybe one of those would work."

George and the Gulls followed me to the shed, but halfway there, George's phone rang. He pulled it out of his pocket to look at the number. "You go on ahead. I have to take this," he said. "It's the boat."

We found the screens and brought the cleanest one over to Gull's front doorway and fitted it in place. It was a little short, but it would do. "Make sure he doesn't chew on the top," I said. "See how it's a little rusty there? Maybe you could wrap a beach towel around it."

I left the Gulls installing a second screen across the back door to the deck, and headed back over to George. I had to finish it now, while we had a minute alone.

George was just snapping his phone shut when I got there. "I have to go," he said. "Emergency at the boat."

"The bilge pump?"

"Yeah, but worse. Electrical fire. Johnny Baker's in the emergency room with second-degree burns. I don't know any more. I've got to go down there now, and I'll be back . . ." He looked at the mower and then his watch. "I don't know when I'll be back. Did that screen do the trick?"

"It did," I said.

"Good job. You know, you fit in here. You can think on your feet, and you don't get too riled up. Louise must be so glad you're here. And so am I. This year, I don't know what I would have done if you weren't here, with Louise laid up and all. Well, I'd better be off to the boat."

"Don't worry about anything here," I said. I suddenly felt elated, like I could lift right off the ground. "We'll take care of everything. You can count on us."

George turned. "I know that. I always do." Then he hurried into his truck. A cloud of dust and shells spat up as he spun away.

I ran back into our house. "Angel!" I yelled, pounding up the stairs, hoping I wasn't too late.

She was there at the foot of her bed, folding T-shirts into crisp origami packets. "You told him?"

"Nope," I said. "We can't go. He needs us."

The smile on Angel's face got wider and wider as I explained. "He really needs us," she agreed. "And it's not like Louise is going to get any . . ."

"No. A little longer won't make a difference to Louise."

"How long?"

"I don't know. Until he doesn't need us, I guess."

"Perfect," Angel said.

I went outside and stood over the mower. I remembered that I'd seen George do three things to start it. I thumbed the rubber button on the top of the handle a bunch of times like he had, flipped the choke lever forward, and then leaned over and gave that starter cord the yank of its life. The mower roared up, startling a cloud of blue butterflies and a pair of crows and filling the air with the smell of gasoline. The smell of going somewhere I'd never been before.

I discovered I liked mowing. Seeing the lawn grow neater, stripe by stripe—as if I were ironing wide green ribbons with the mower—calmed me down the way cleaning did. It helped me see things clearly. And what I saw was this: It didn't matter that my mom and I weren't going to inherit this house. Louise hadn't owned it either, and yet it was hers. It was hers because she kept it clean, because she had painted the cabinets yellow, because she baked pies in it and grew a garden beside it and tended those blueberry bushes. She'd tied herself to this place.

I'd been tying myself to this place too, and so it felt like mine. I'd been taking care of the cottages, and the blueberry patch, and the families who came to stay, and now here I was mowing the lawn. I'd tied myself to all of it.

And then something struck me—so obvious I couldn't believe I'd missed it: The person George hired to replace Louise was going to have everything that mattered.

I knew who that person had to be. I just had to get her the job.

George called that night, and I was ready.

"Oh, right. Bingo. With Anita," he said when I told him Louise wasn't home. I didn't disagree.

"When she gets back, you tell her I've got a big mess on my hands. I've got to tear out the fried wiring and replace it, then put in a new pump. Johnny Baker's going to be fine, but I need to find someone to fill in for him for a week or two, train him to the gear. . . . I won't be available much.

I'll send someone over to finish the mowing."

"I already did it," I said. "George, guess what? My mother's coming here soon—"

"You did it? You mean you mowed the lawn?"

"Yep, but about my mother—"

"You got the mower started? You gotta be strong to do that. Don't tell me you were wearing those flip-flops!"

"No. Sneakers." I sighed. This was going to be trickier than I'd hoped.

"Boots are better. And long pants, always—the mower chips up stones and shells all the time. Tell me you wore long pants."

"Shorts," I admitted.

"Well," he said. "As long as you're all right. Next time, though: boots and long pants. And safety glasses—don't want you to lose an eye. But thank you. You're a one, Stella by Starlight. You're a one. Oh, hey, I almost forgot. You wanted to tell me something about Louise."

"Oh, I . . . it's not important. Never mind. But George . . . you know, my mom's going to be coming here pretty soon. By the end of the summer."

"That so?"

From just those two words, I knew that Louise had told him some things about my mother, and that none of them were good.

"She used to be kind of flighty, I know, but she's doing much better now. Really responsible."

"That's good. Well, thanks again for the mowing. You're a one, all right."

"Wait. It's been tough, you know," I said in a rush. "I mean, can you imagine? Losing your father when you're little, then your mother, then not having a place to live. . . ."

"I do think that's tough," he said slowly, as if he had to choose each word carefully. "I said so to Louise when she told me."

"She told you how hard it's been for my mom?" I hadn't expected this.

"Your mom? No, she was talking about . . ."

There was a long silence, but I heard the word that George didn't say. "Me?" My voice was so small, I almost didn't recognize it. "What did Louise say about me?" I asked, bigger and louder.

I heard George sigh. "All right," he said after another long pause. "Exact words. She said, 'That girl doesn't have a father or a mother or a home. She needs some taking care of, and I'm the one who's meant to do it.'"

When I hung up with George, I went to my room, closed the door, and lay down on my bed. Everything Louise had told George was true—I didn't have a father or a mother or a home right now—but it still didn't seem to have much to do with me.

My home—my grandmother's home—well, I used to miss that. A lot. But since coming to Louise's, I hadn't.

And I didn't actually miss my parents.

My mother? All my life, she'd been coming and going. She'd be back soon, because the court told her to take those classes and get us a home. She always came back.

And I didn't miss my father, because you can't miss someone you don't remember—I'd been only two when he left, and two-year-olds aren't known for their great memories. My mother refused to talk about him, and I only found out the two things I knew about him—that he played the trombone and that he had named me—by accident.

I closed my eyes to replay the memory. A lady had come to visit my mother. I was fascinated with her fingernails—they were long and painted a silvery purple. My mother had shooed me inside and plopped me in front of the television, turned up loud, then joined the lady out on the porch, carrying a pitcher of something frosty and pink. I could still hear them laughing and talking over the program.

"So what do you hear from your trumpet player?" Silver Nails asked, and something in my four-year-old self knew to pay attention. I slipped over to the window and listened.

"Trombone player," my mother said. "And wasn't that

just perfect? He thought he could slide in and out of my life, in and out like a trombone, leaving nothing but pretty music."

"Does he ever try to see . . ." Somehow I knew Silver Nails was tilting her head inside, toward me.

"Uh-uh. I didn't even tell him we were moving up here. Why bother? The limit of his fathering skills was naming her."

"He named her? Oh, I wondered," said Silver Nails.

"Some old-time song he knew. 'Stella by Starlight.' Said it was his favorite. I suppose it could have been worse— he also loved one called 'Minnie the Moocher.' Huh . . . Stella!" The way my mother said it that afternoon, my name felt like a slap to my cheek. "Stella is burdensome enough—I don't think I could take having a kid named Minnie!" Then they clinked their glasses and howled like that was a good one.

I wasn't laughing, though. I couldn't have known what the word "burdensome" meant at four, but my heart hurt from it all the same.

Now, I sat up as it occurred to me: Katie Sandpiper was four—exactly the age I had been then. I got up and knelt by the window and looked down over the cottages. I tried to imagine Katie listening to her mother howling with laughter over her name, saying things like that about her father. Even when I pictured Katie in my old house instead of the perfect cottage below me, I couldn't imagine it.

And then I realized something. These perfect cottages didn't make the families happy. It was the other way around: The happy families made my cottages perfect. That was the magic.

I went back to my bed. I lay very still and called up my movie, because just then I really needed to picture my mother peaceful and happy to be home here with me. I closed my eyes and rolled it out: my mother coming into Louise's kitchen, hanging her jacket over the chair and sighing. But a weird thing happened. My mother still wore the "I won the daughter lottery and I'm staying right where I am" smile, but this time, *she* was the one at the stove, and *I* was the one leaning in to see what was cooking. And the pot was full of orange food.

CHAPTER ◇ 23 ◇

"We eat relish," Angel said from her perch on the counter Monday morning. "Relish and Froot Loops dust. It's crazy that we're so happy to be here."

It wasn't crazy, though. Now we belonged here, because George was counting on us, because he needed us. And maybe we were happy because somehow Angel and I had become friends.

"Do you ever wonder what it would be like if Louise hadn't died?" I asked. "I mean, I wish she were still alive, of course. But if she hadn't died, do you think you and I would still be . . . oil and water?"

"Maybe," Angel said. "It's too hard to think about, because everything is different now."

I agreed. Everything was different now, and the difference was that it all felt right.

Except that we were starving.

In the afternoon, I tried the pizza trick again.

This time, Mama herself answered. I gave her the order, read her the card number, then told her our address.

"Pickup only. Delivery kid quit. Teenagers . . . hey, how old are you anyway?"

I hung up. When I told Angel what had happened, she leaped up as though it was exactly the news she'd been waiting for. She grabbed Louise's car keys from the hook and jangled them in front of me. "Let's go get that pizza."

"Are you crazy?" I cried. "We'd be arrested in a minute."

"No," Angel insisted. "I've been practicing in the driveway. I'm really good now."

"Even if you could drive, somebody would see a kid driving and call the police."

Angel smiled. "Wait here."

I had to laugh: Angel came back wearing one of Louise's flowery blouses, and she had painted big red lips on. I stopped laughing when she tucked her hair up under Louise's straw gardening hat. It could work.

"Well, you really can drive?" I said. "Show me."

We got into the car and buckled up. Angel clicked the key into the ignition and the engine started smoothly, which I thought was a good sign. She looked over her shoulder before she backed up, which I thought was another good sign. She winked at me and stepped on the gas.

The car leaped. Forward into the privet hedge. We bucked to a stop.

"Cancel that idea," I said. I went inside and sat at the kitchen table to think. Angel came in and hung up the key without a word. She pulled up a chair beside me.

"We can't get to a store and we can't order pizza and it's five more days until changeover," I said.

"Why isn't there a restaurant around here? Why do we have to live in the middle of nowhere?"

"Well, actually, there is," I said. "It's on a side street near the beach." I'd noticed the sign walking home one day and checked it out, hoping they'd have a Dumpster outside—restaurants threw out a lot of perfectly good food. The restaurant was in an old captain's house. It had a widow's walk and a wide porch and a whale weathervane, but no Dumpster. "But it's fancy."

"We'll change our clothes," Angel said. She looked down at Louise's blouse. "Or I can keep it on. . . ."

I shook my head. "The menu was in a glass case outside. The cheapest thing is sixteen dollars."

"Let's go," Angel said. "I'd pay sixteen dollars for a meal today."

"It was a salad, Angel. Probably three bites of something you wouldn't eat. Besides, a place like that isn't going to let two kids come in without asking questions."

And then I had an idea. "Do you know how to fish?"

I watched Angel's face carefully, but she seemed all right with the word. "No," she admitted. "But . . . how about clams? We could dig clams."

We grabbed a wire basket from the shed, and twenty minutes later, Angel and I were out on the flats at the end of Mill River Beach with the regular clammers. Including the boy.

"Now what?" Angel asked.

"We do what they're doing, I guess." I got to my knees and started scooping sand with my hands, making a pile beside me, just like I'd seen the clammers do so many times. I dug and dug, but I never ran into a clam.

"You're scaring them," Angel said. "You should sneak up on them."

I looked around. Nobody seemed to be sneaking up

on anything. Clammer boy was sitting back on his heels, watching us. "We're clamming," I called over to him, my idiot mouth taking over. "We're going to make chowder. For our family."

Angel elbowed me to shut up, but it was no use—my blabber instinct had kicked in full power. "They're waiting for us at home. Our family. Waiting for the clams. To make the chowder."

Clammer boy got up and rinsed his hands in the water, then walked over to us. "These are the wrong clams." He looked more closely at the heaps of sand around me. "Well, if you'd found any, they'd be the wrong clams."

"What are you talking about, the wrong clams?" Angel asked, her hands on her hips, as if he'd insulted her.

"These are soft-shelled. Steamers. You want quahogs." He waved at the inlet. "Over there."

"Under the *water*?" Angel asked.

He nodded. "You need a rake."

"No, we don't," Angel snapped. "Our family likes a special kind of chowder. Made with *these* clams. Can you just show us how to catch them?"

Clammer boy looked like he was about to set Angel straight about soft-shelled clams, but one look at her face convinced him that would be a bad idea. He dropped to his knees and forked his fingers into the wet sand. "Go in slow, so you don't cut yourself on anything, then scoop out fast. There are plenty of holes here, which means plenty of clams. You just didn't go deep enough." He dug a hole the size of a basketball. "Now feel around for a smooth tip. . . . There's one!" He tunneled his fingers in deeper and tugged out a gray-and-white oval clam. "Anything under two inches, put it back."

"Great, got it!" said Angel. "We can do it now, thanks!"

He left, and I felt sad for a moment. Which was ridiculous. Then Angel and I got to work. It felt good to kneel in the wet, gritty sand and pull out clams. The sun was warm on my back through my shirt, and the sounds of gulls and waves wove themselves into a kind of song. I noticed Angel never looked up to gaze at the water the way I did, but on the other hand, she didn't seem all that eager to leave. After maybe forty-five minutes, our basket was full of clams, and Angel and I were full of new hope.

"There was some cream left in Plover," I said, walking back down the beach. "And onions in the garden. I really could make chowder."

"Or fried clams," Angel said, dreamily. "I love those. *Jesus querido,* we are saved!"

Halfway back, we came upon a flock of gulls sitting on a narrow bar of sand. "Angel," I said, pointing. "That thing you did, where you lifted your arms . . ."

Angel nodded. "And they flew. My father taught me."

"How do you do it?"

Angel shrugged. "I get as close as they'll let me, then I pretend I'm one of them. And I think, 'Let's fly,' and I raise my wings." She dropped her head. "Never mind—that sounds stupid. Just sneak up on them, then raise your arms."

"Show me," I asked.

Angel shook her head and took the basket of clams from me. "You."

So very slowly, step by step, I walked through the shallows to the sandbar. One step up onto the bar, though, and the birds shifted. I stopped. The birds resettled. And then I spread my arms high, as if my hands suddenly needed to burst into flight. I thought to those birds, *Let's fly!*

And they did! Just like when Angel had done it, all the gulls rose at once, their wings taking flight with my arms. I turned to grin at Angel.

She gave me a smile back, but it was half sad. "Every time I do it," she said, "I'm always sort of disappointed I don't fly up with them. That they leave me and I'm always stuck here on the ground."

She laughed then, and we each took a side of the bucket's handle and lifted our heavy dinner. We walked the rest of the way down the beach, talking about nothing much. It felt so good, I even made a joke about it. "Have you noticed we're *talking*, Angel?" I said. "I saw something like this on an episode of *Friends* once." And Angel even laughed at that, after she fake-punched my arm.

When we got to the stretch of sand next to the parking lot, we were still talking. Neither of us paid much attention to the man in the tan uniform who emerged from a van and walked toward us.

"Evening, girls." He tapped a badge on his shirt pocket. "Shellfish warden. Looks like you've got yourself a nice mess of clams. Could I see your license?"

"License?" Angel and I asked together.

He nodded. "You need a shellfish license to take clams. Guess you're not from around here, are you?"

"We live in Spring Valley," Angel said. "Both of us. It's in . . . New Jersey."

"Well, tell your parents that here on Cape Cod you need a permit before you can go clamming."

"Okay, we will. Thanks, officer." Angel turned for the road.

"Not so fast," the warden called. "I'm afraid I'll

have to take those."

Angel hesitated. She looked at the road, and I could see her weighing the odds of making a run for it. I admit that the hungry part of me wanted her to try. But then she tipped the clams out on the wet sand at her feet.

"Say," she said. "Since we're tourists and all, could you tell me what that island is over there?" She pointed out to sea.

The warden turned and shaded his eyes from the lowering sun. "That'd be Monomoy Island. Too hazy today, but if it were clear, you could see Nantucket a little to the west, right about where that trawler is. . . . You see it?"

But Angel had already set out for the parking lot, swinging our empty basket. I trudged after her, thinking the whole way home about my empty stomach.

When we got there, I collapsed onto the back steps. "I'm too weak to go inside."

Angel stood in front of me, patting her hips with a funny look. She lifted the hem of her tee and drew something out of her shorts pocket.

A clam. And then another. And another.

One by one, she pulled eleven clams out and laid them beside me on the step. She spread her hands in mock shock. "Go figure. They must have jumped in while Officer Friendly was showing me Nantucket."

We boiled those eleven clams. They tasted like salty rubber bands coated in sand. Delicious.

Afterward, Angel went out to toss the shells into the driveway. When she walked back in the door, I really looked at her. Her nails were ragged and blackened. Her hair looked like it hadn't been brushed in a week. Worst of all, her shorts were hanging off her hipbones.

Angel and I were three weeks starving and dirty. And no one had noticed. Wasn't someone supposed to notice?

CHAPTER

◇ 24 ◇

Thursday morning, I woke up stuck to the sheets in sweat. It must have been over ninety, and the sun was just up. The renters had only a few quick questions about where the water was coldest, and everybody was gone by ten.

"I saw an air conditioner in Louise's closet," Angel remembered. "Under her four hundred shoes." She went up to check and came back down again in a few minutes. "It weighs a thousand pounds—I think we're just going to have to boil today. But I found this." She held out a brown grocery bag. "It has your name on it."

Angel left to stand in a cold shower. I opened the bag.

A package with a UPS label. Whatever was inside bumped in the box like a solid thing with corners. A book. I opened it, and my heart caught: a brand-new copy of *Heloise from A to Z*. This was the actual dictionary of household hints. I opened the cover, and the spine cracked, it was so full of new promise. And inside, handwritten, were these words:

> For Stella.
> Happy birthday and happy hinting.
> Heloise.

I stared at that page for a long, long time.

Then I picked up the chair Angel used to give her soap opera report and went out to the garden. I settled the chair in a patch of shade beside Louise.

"Hey, Louise," I said. "Did you ever notice how I used to do that? Say 'hey' in front of your name—'Hey, Louise'—and I'd slide the words together to make it sound like Heloise? I want you to know it was a compliment. I really like Heloise. And I think you were like her. Thank you so much—that book is the best present."

It was sweltering out there, but I didn't want to go in. I leaned over and plucked out a few weeds. "Hey, Louise,"

I said again. "I'm sorry about what I thought—that you were taking care of us just for the money. I should have known better. I mean, you're a gardener. Nobody pays you to take care of these plants. You probably figured Angel and I got planted with you, and you were going to take care of us, and make sure we had everything we needed. You were probably looking forward to seeing what we sprouted into.

"Are you okay out here? I really hope we did the right thing—I thought it would be your favorite place, next to your blueberry bushes. I wish you could see them. They're doing really well now, finally, but I've had to work so hard. George helped—he was the one who told me about the gypsy moths. He really did love your pies, you know. For a while, Angel thought he was in love with you."

I fanned myself for a minute, thinking about how nice it would have been if George and Louise *had* been boyfriend and girlfriend, keeping each other company. "Well," I said finally, "thank you again for the present. You couldn't have picked anything better, and I really appreciate how you thought ahead and got it signed."

As I got up, I heard a window creak open above me. Angel craned her head out. "You can just leave the chair out there, you know," she said.

I went inside and stacked the dishes in the dishwasher and wiped down the counters, moving in slow motion because of the heat. Then I decided it was my birthday, and I should quit working early.

I brought my new book up to my room to place it next to my Hints file, to read when I got home from the beach. But it was missing. My folder of Hints from Heloise, the only thing I had from my grandmother, was missing.

I felt a panic rise in me so powerful, it was hard to take a breath. I flew around the house, looking everywhere. The kitchen, the living room, the den, even the bathrooms.

Finally I banged open Angel's door. She sat in the mess of her bed, pulling her earphones out. "What?"

"My hints!" I cried. I heard the quaver in my voice, but I didn't care. "They're gone. You have to help me find them. Someone must have—"

I stopped short.

There was my Hints folder, on top of Angel's bureau. I ran over and grabbed it and clutched it to my chest. Then I turned to face her. "You took it? Why?"

Angel stared at me. She pressed her lips closed, and then she put her earphones back in and closed her eyes.

I stormed out. Back in my own room, I went through

my hints. They were all there, and all still in order. I read over some of them and my breathing slowed. Still.

How stupid I'd been to think maybe we were becoming friends! Six more weeks until Labor Day. Wherever that girl was, I wasn't. Back to where we started.

I went to my bed with my new dictionary of hints, pulled a sheet over me even though it was about a hundred degrees, and started with A.

CHAPTER

◇ 25 ◇

That afternoon, Mrs. Sandpiper called me to babysit.

"Daniel has a ball game in Wareham, and it's just too hot to make Katie sit in the stands all afternoon," she said when I got there. "She's a little minnow this week. Take her to Mill River Beach and she'll be happy."

"Oh," I said. "The thing is, I'm not a lifeguard."

"That's okay. We were there this morning. She only flops around in the shallows. It's so hot." Mrs. Sandpiper pooched her mouth in the mirror and slicked on some coral lipstick. At her waist, Katie mimicked the pooching, and Mrs. Sandpiper dabbed a spot of lipstick on her lips.

I had to close my eyes—sometimes when I saw mothers and daughters, it felt like I was being stung by a hot, bright light.

"I don't know," I said. "Maybe we could stay here?"

Katie raised her eyebrows and hung her painted mouth open in shock that I could even consider not going to the beach.

"It'll be fine," Mrs. Sandpiper said. "Katie, you're not to go out over your knees, you got that?" She stroked a lipstick line across each of Katie's little knees. "That's the mark, okay? You do what Stella tells you."

Katie nodded so hard her fountain-head flopped over. So I said okay to the beach and told myself there was nothing to worry about. Katie and I waved good-bye to her family, then packed up and hiked down to the beach.

I walked her all the way down to the last jetty, taking our time even though the air was like steam and the cool water called. "How about we make a sand castle?" I suggested. Katie ignored me and headed straight for the water. I caught her hand. "Look," I said, pointing to a line of birds tottering on their toothpick legs along the water's edge. "Sandpipers. Those are the birds your cottage is named after." I swept my palm upward, where the sky was full of birds. "Those big ones are gulls. And the smaller ones are terns. Like the other cottages. I wonder if we can find some plovers. . . ."

Katie couldn't be distracted with birds. She tugged on my hand.

"And look," I tried. "Way down there, to the west. The sky looks dark there, like it might be raining. We shouldn't stay too long, in case Daniel's game gets canceled."

Katie tugged harder. She wasn't going to buy anything I offered. I dumped our stuff and let her drag me into the water. And her mother was right—all Katie wanted to do was splash around in the shallows.

After a while, I plunked myself down near her and leaned back on my elbows to watch. Each time one of the tiny waves slapped me on the belly, I laughed at the cold splash, but I still wished we weren't here. Weeks ago, when Angel was yelling about my rules, she said I must have a hundred rules about swimming. And she was right. Always face the waves—that way you know what's coming. Never swim at night—jellyfish and other dangers are hard to see in the dark. Never swim alone. Never swim on an outgoing tide. The ocean was unpredictable. It helped to have some rules.

In front of me, Katie draped a hank of seaweed over her head and laughed so hard she fell over backward. I jumped to my feet, but she was up and laughing in a second. Four years old, that kid had no fear. She was like Angel that way.

So different from me.

And that's when I felt the alarm bells at the back of my neck. I stood up and looked around. Katie was dog-paddling in a circle in front of me. A dozen kids were splashing around in the waist-high water. Families all around me were reading and eating and dozing. Everyone was fine. It was a sunny day at the beach, and everyone was fine.

The alarm bells shrilled louder. It didn't make sense. No one had left me.

I took a few steps up the beach, but there was nothing to see. I walked back to the water. "Katie," I called. "Come in."

A woman walking the shore in a red suit stopped. She waved to a little boy in the water, then looked at me.

"Katie! Come out of the water. Now."

Katie stood up and cocked her head at me, trying to decide if I was serious.

"What is it?" the woman asked.

"Do you have all your kids?" I asked. I didn't care how foolish I sounded.

The woman just stared at me. I turned back to Katie. "Hurry up, Kate."

Other parents rose and came to the shoreline, alert to something in my voice. "Bring them in," I told them.

"What?" the woman in the red suit asked.

She was at least a foot taller than I was, but somehow it felt like I was looking into her eyes on a level. "I don't know," I said. "But I'm never wrong when I get this feeling. Bring them in."

I rushed out and took Katie by the wrist. "Justin," I heard the woman in the red suit call. "Come in now, honey." The other parents started calling in their kids nervously.

And suddenly I understood why I felt someone was missing: The sky was empty of birds. I scanned the horizon. The wall of clouds in the west had gathered itself into a ball, blacker and much closer now. And rolling—tumbling over itself, it was coming so fast, like a bowling ball hurled down the curve of the coast. "Look. There." I pointed to it, and just as I did, a thread of lightning sizzled down from the thunderheads and danced a second on the sea.

I got Katie to the towels and dried her off, counting to the first muffled clap of thunder. The storm was about three miles away. Parents were running into the water now, grabbing their kids, splashing back to shore.

I tugged Katie's T-shirt and sneakers on, stuffed everything else into the beach bag. The sky grew darker suddenly, and a cool wind gusted up, chopping into the water, which had turned the color of steel. Around us, the other families were gathering themselves, hurrying.

I glanced up and saw another silver bolt snake through

the sky, jagged as broken glass. The crack of thunder followed right away—this storm meant business. "Hurry up, kidlet." I took Katie's hand and pulled her along as fast as her little legs could go.

Halfway to the parking lot, it began to rain—fat, cold drops that seemed to be in a hurry to get to the ground before the big show. The wind picked up against us. The rain was pelting down so hard now that each drop sent shots of sand spattering our calves.

"It's biting me!" Katie cried.

"Faster, Katie, hurry."

At the parking lot, families who had been at the nearer jetties were already piling into cars and peeling out. I hurried Katie up the road, the rain sheeting down now so that it was hard to see. We ducked into the woods, where the rain poured off the leaves in drenching curtains and the trees shook with each thunderclap. The pine needles and sand made a slippery muck and Katie kept falling, so I scooped her into my arms and scrambled up the path behind the cottages.

In the clearing, the air around us felt like a solid living thing, glimmering a sick yellow through the rain. It suddenly split in two right above us with a crack so loud, I thought my rib cage had exploded. A pine branch crashed to the ground behind us. Katie screamed and dug her fingers into my neck, and I flat-out raced across the yard to Sandpiper. And only as I pulled out the key did I recognize it from every illustration of Ben Franklin discovering electricity the hard way. I dropped Katie, opened the door, and threw the key down, then grabbed her again and tumbled with her to the couch.

I got Katie into dry clothes, and we watched the storm. It was over quickly, racing away as fast as it had come in. Afterward, Katie wouldn't leave my side. A branch had broken a windowpane in the kitchen, and she sat on her hands on the counter, perfectly still, while I pulled out the shards of glass and taped in a square of cardboard I'd cut from a Wheaties box. Even though the sun came out, she didn't want to go outside, so we settled on the couch with grilled cheese sandwiches and played Candy Land, her hand curled in mine.

"She was the first one! Nobody else saw it!" Katie told her parents over and over when they got home.

Katie's mother couldn't stop thanking me. "We heard about the storm and raced home as fast as we could. We were so afraid you were stuck at the beach." When she paid me, she gave me an extra twenty. "It doesn't begin to thank you," she said. "I really can't thank you enough for being so responsible. I'm sure you make your family very proud."

* * *

It was like a different day—the sun was low and the air was cool now, and so clear that on the horizon I could see a humped shape that must be Nantucket. I walked across the yard, covered now with branches and leaves, wishing I wasn't so mad at Angel—I wanted to tell someone about my day.

No. I wanted to tell *Angel* about it.

When I got inside, the living room was dark. At first I thought the storm had knocked out the power, but no, it was just that the shades were down. I closed the door behind me, and Angel stepped out of the shadows.

"Happy birthday to you," she sang. Her face was beaming in the light of twelve wooden matches planted in the frosting of a cake. "I made it yesterday when you were at the beach. Mrs. Plover picked up the stuff at the store for me," Angel said in a rush. "It's just a mix and the frosting's canned, so I thought, Hey, that's easy, I can handle it. But look—it's all crooked and saggy. That's why I took your Heloise folder. I'm sorry. I was looking for a hint to fix it, but I couldn't tell you, because it would ruin the surprise."

"Oh, Angel . . . thank you!" I stared between Angel's face, grinning with pride, and the cake she'd made, feeling stupid because I couldn't come up with the words I really wanted to say. "Thank you," I said again. "Thank you, Angel!"

Angel pulled me into the kitchen and sat me at the table. She had set it with Louise's good china and silver, and a vase of roses and daylilies. She filled two crystal wineglasses with water and cut two big slices of cake. Her smile fell. "It's all soupy inside. I messed it up—it's not cooked enough...."

"No, it's good that way. I hate dry cake. And it's not your fault. Louise's oven is out of whack—it runs cool," I lied. "I should have told you."

Angel's face relaxed, and we ate the cake. And it was good—really good—like cake with batter in it.

"Angel," I said, as we sat at the table licking the last frosting off our forks, "you're always acting so tough, like you don't care. About George, about Louise, about me. But then you do these things...." I raised my hands to the cake and the flowers. "You're such a Yankee!"

Angel put her fork down, wary. "What's that supposed to mean?"

Before I could answer, the phone rang. We both jumped. Angel snatched it up. "No, we're fine. Yep, we have power." She mouthed "George" at me and flicked some pretend sweat from her forehead.

"Tell him a kitchen window broke in Sandpiper. We

need a pane of glass."

Angel did, and then she listened some more. "No, you just missed her. Ah . . . them. You just missed her and her boyfriend." Whatever the response was made her squeeze her eyes shut, as though it hurt to hear it. "Well, how about you just mail it, okay? . . . No . . . Well, okay, see you soon."

She hung up and swore. "He's on his way over. Some papers that won't wait." Angel spread her hands.

"We'd better clean up."

She looked around the kitchen. Her gaze rested on the fancy china and wineglasses on the table. "Or not. . . ."

"What do you mean?"

"Okay, maybe he's not in love with her. But we still need him to believe in Louise's boyfriend." Angel ran out the back door, and I heard her clang open the recycling bin.

She came back again carrying an empty wine bottle. She placed it on the table next to the glasses, then dashed upstairs and came down with a can of hairspray and a tube of Louise's lipstick. Hairspray clouded the kitchen. "Best I could do. No perfume." Then she smeared some lipstick on and pressed one of the glasses to her mouth a couple of times. She held the glass up and nodded. "Okay, now for the last touch."

Angel left one more time, and came back with the cigar that had been in Mr. Gull's suit jacket. She lit a match to one end, ran the other under the faucet, then laid the cigar on one of the cake plates. "What a slob. I don't know what Louise sees in him. Okay, does it look like they've had a romantic evening?"

"Let's hope so," I said. "Because George just pulled in."

From the minute he walked in, it was clear he wasn't in any mood to hear about Louise's romance. He dropped a letter onto the table. "You girls give her this and have her call me as soon as she gets in."

"She might be out pretty late." Angel picked up a wineglass and studied it. "It's amazing she left this much lipstick on here, with the amount of kissing they were doing."

George tapped the letter. "The Board of Appeals says they never got our petition. They sent the paperwork a month ago, and she was supposed to have it in last week. The Zoning Committee meets on the twenty-fifth. This isn't like her."

"She's been pretty confused lately . . . ," Angel tried. "What with her boyfriend turning up after all these years."

"Pretty confused? Something's going on with her. Something's not right." He picked up the letter again and flipped it back down. "I'll be back Saturday. No need to mow, it's been so hot, but I'll come for the trash and I'll fix that window. You tell her I'm going to need those forms by then."

George left, and Angel and I stood at the open door, watching his taillights flicker away.

Once we found the forms George's letter was referring to in the mail basket, it wasn't actually that hard: square footage of the cottages, distance to the wetlands, number of bathrooms, annual rental income. I did the math while Angel practiced Louise's handwriting; then she filled in the numbers I gave her.

"Why are you bothering to figure it all out?" she asked. "All that matters is that it's filled in, so George doesn't freak out."

"I guess so," I said. But I checked and rechecked everything carefully, and I made sure that by the time we sealed up the envelope, every number was right.

Late that night, the phone woke me. I ignored the ringing, concentrating on listening for the rustle that meant Angel was where she should be. But when the message began to record, I shot upright. My mother's voice.

I raced out of bed and halfway down the stairs, then remembered the extension in Louise's room and ran up a couple of steps, then back down when I remembered we'd unplugged it last week. By the time I skidded into the kitchen, the phone was silent and blinking. I hit play and knelt beside the machine.

"Happy birthday, baby, it's Mom! I can't believe you're twelve. . . . I feel ancient! I've got a present you're going to love. Well, I guess you're out celebrating with Louise, so I'll talk to you on Saturday. I miss you. Bye!"

I played the message three times. "Happy birthday, baby. . . . I'll talk to you on Saturday." As if she had remembered to call every week. I was just about to erase it, but then I thought about how much I had changed and how much Angel had changed. Maybe my mother had changed, too. It was important to stay positive. My mother could change, too.

CHAPTER
26

Friday was hot again, although clear, not sticky. The renters all pulled out early again, and I headed out to check on my blueberry bushes. Even with the heat, they were looking really good now. In just one week they'd popped out new green leaves and were sprinkled with berries that were actually turning blue.

After I'd weeded in the garden for a while, I went inside to ask Angel if she wanted to come with me to the beach—try a quick swimming lesson. She just rolled her eyes and turned the fan up to high and flipped on the television.

"Today's the day. That Lorraine M. person will probably

call when Louise doesn't show up," I reminded her. "Let the machine get it, or give her some story."

By noon, I was floating on my back, rocking in the cool waves, thinking about what I should tell my mother when she called the next day. Whatever it took, I needed to get her here so George could meet her. The parenting courses were a couple of weeks long, I remembered, so she needed to come back by the middle of August anyway, but I wanted her back sooner. Maybe Mrs. Marino had been wrong about not pressing her. Maybe it was exactly what she needed.

I thrashed upright with a gasp, swallowing salt water, when it hit me.

Mrs. Marino's first name was Lorraine. I'd seen it on her desk once—Lorraine Marino. *Lorraine M.*

I grabbed my stuff and raced home. A red car was parked behind Louise's, the engine still ticking.

I hurried inside. She was there, standing with Angel. I went weak all over, as if my strength had leaked out through the soles of my feet.

"Remember Mrs. Marino, from Family Services?" Angel asked, a fake smile plastered over her face, which was sand-dollar white. "I was just explaining to her that Louise must have forgotten she was coming."

"We've had this visit scheduled for a month," Mrs. Marino said.

"There was an emergency," Angel said. "Her niece called, all hysterical. Louise went to give her some advice. She's the heart of the town, you know. Everybody comes to her with their problems."

"Does she have a cell phone?" Mrs. Marino interrupted.

"No, she doesn't like them," I answered.

This part was true anyway. "Why would I want to give people a way to bother me when I don't want to be bothered?" were her exact words on the subject.

"Does she leave you alone often?" Mrs. Marino pulled out a notebook and jotted something down. I figured it wasn't a good report about Louise.

"No," I said. "Besides, we're old enough. I'm twelve now. And she remembered my birthday. She just forgot this one thing."

"Mrs. Marino, would you like some coffee cake? There's some in the freezer. Louise is always prepared," Angel said, flashing her a lot of teeth.

"Or some of my birthday cake?" I added. "It's delicious."

The Family Services woman looked confused for a minute, as if she knew she was being sidetracked but she couldn't see exactly where. "Well, that would be nice. You girls could tell me how you're getting along."

She sat at the table, and I plowed through the mail basket

for my mom's postcard while Angel got some dishes out. It was still there, tucked into the Humane Society brochure. I held it out. "My mom's been in touch a lot. See? She's getting a job. She's going to be back soon for those classes, of course."

Angel carried over my cake and set it on the table. I caught Mrs. Marino's face when she got a look at it with its lopsided layers and runny middle and twelve matches for candles. "Oh, on second thought . . . ," she said, backpedaling.

And something snapped. "This is a *beautiful* cake," I told her. "This is the best cake anyone's ever made me."

"Oh, well of course it is. . . . She took the time to make a cake for you. That means a lot."

"Yes it does," I said, sliding a quick look at Angel. "It means a lot when someone makes you a cake. So you should be reporting that in your notebook, not anything bad about Louise."

Mrs. Marino set her jaw and didn't answer. "We'll have to reschedule this." She thumbed through her notebook. "The thirtieth would work for me, in the afternoon. I'll give her a call Monday to confirm."

She left, and Angel and I sank to the kitchen chairs, our heads in our hands, our backs rivered with sweat that was only partly from the heat. When we could breathe normally, I looked across at Angel.

Stop, Access, Think. "Emergency meeting, Angel," I said. "What are we going to do? The thirtieth's not for a week and a half. Can we stay? Do you still want to? We have to decide this together—equal votes, remember?"

Angel got up and propped the refrigerator door open. The cool air helped calm my panic. She turned to me. "My aunt's got a job cleaning. She doesn't have an apartment yet. But soon."

"What about the money? Do you have enough?"

Angel got up and counted it. "About two hundred thirty now, with this week's babysitting. Maybe another sixty in tips tomorrow." Angel calculated. "A hundred forty-five each. Almost halfway there."

"What do you need it for, anyway?" I asked. Not that I expected Angel would actually tell me.

She went over and stuck her head in the freezer. Then she turned to me, raising her arms to chill them in the cold air streaming out. It reminded me of how she'd made the birds lift on the beach. How she always half wished they would take her with them.

"My mother had a guitar," she said. "A fado guitar, called a Coimbra, made in Portugal. Very beautiful, very valuable. It got broken in the crash that . . ." Angel took Louise's coffee cake out and pressed it to her forehead with her eyes closed. Then she put it back and started again. "She was coming home from singing. She'd stopped at the market, and she had a bag of groceries on the seat beside her. It was so weird—the groceries didn't even spill. There were eggs in the bag. She was going to dye them for my first Easter. Not a single egg was broken.

"When I was little, everyone told me that story, like it was supposed to mean something. 'The eggs were fine! But the neck of her guitar was broken! And she was . . .' I don't think it meant anything, and I just wanted them all to shut up about the stupid eggs. But I need to have that guitar fixed. There's a man in Lisbon who can do it. He's going to charge me two hundred dollars, but I have to pack it a special way in a crate he's going to build and ship over here. Then it gets shipped to him to fix, then shipped back. . . . It's three hundred fifty dollars for everything." She took a long breath and blew it out in a cloud into the freezer. She shut the door. "My mother's guitar is broken. It was really special to her. I need to fix it."

Of course, I knew what I should say to her. I knew I should tell her what George had told me about broken things. I knew I should tell her that she didn't have to fix that guitar, because it told a story. But I didn't, because I realized that if she didn't want the money anymore, she might leave. My heart cramped up, and I didn't tell her what I should have.

"I think we can make it two more changeovers," I said. "There should be enough money then—you can take three hundred fifty and I'll take what's left. And I will get my mother here by then, so George can meet her and see that she could take Louise's job here."

"Why don't you just tell him about her?"

For a minute, I didn't know how to explain it. Then my eyes landed on the Humane Society brochure that was still on the table. I handed it to Angel. "Do you think George would have Treb now if he'd just seen his picture in here?"

"What are you talking about? No. You heard the story."

"See, I don't think so either. I think he had to meet Treb to see what a great dog he was. To even get the idea he might want a dog." I folded the flyer, so I didn't have to look at those sad puppy eyes. "George needs to meet my mother, too. I'll get her here next week."

That night, the moon rose in a clear sky, flooding my room with a silver glow, as if something magical was about to happen. It was almost full, reminding me that Louise had died exactly four weeks ago. I went over the things that had happened since then. All the things that had changed. It seemed something was missing—not in an alarm-bells way, just missing. I lay quietly listening for Angel's sleeping sounds and thinking that in a week or so I'd be listening for the little whimper that meant my mom was there, instead.

And that's when I figured out what was missing: For the first time, I didn't hear the gypsy moth caterpillars chewing. That meant they were in their pupae now, growing their wings. In a couple of weeks, they'd emerge. They'd be gypsy moths.

George had called them pests. So had Louise's gardening magazines. I had hated them. But really, what had they done that was so wrong? They'd fed on the leaves in the dark of the night, until they were able to fly.

You had to admire them for that. They did what they needed to do, in the dark so nobody would bother them, getting ready for their big adventure of becoming moths.

I suddenly knew I wasn't going to sleep until I had tried something. I got up and tugged on some clothes. Then I hurried down the stairs and outside, the screen door slapping behind me like a clap of applause.

As I reached the path, I heard a window scrape open.

"Where are you going?" Angel called down.

"It's dark. It's an outgoing tide," I said. "It's something I need to do. Go back to bed."

And then I took off down the path, making my way by the light of the moon. Past the brambles, over the rough turf, down the road to the parking lot. I didn't stop until I got to the head of the beach.

I stood there for what was probably only five minutes but felt like forever. The sky was a vast black bowl, filled with millions of glittering stars. I was what my father had named me now: Stella by Starlight.

Right there, I decided something—someday I would find my father. I would make my mother tell me his name, and I would find him and I would tell him about this night when I was what he named me. I peeled off my clothes and walked to the shoreline.

I heard a voice from the top of the dunes. "Stop! Don't do it! Well, whatever *it* is you're doing. What are you doing, anyway?"

Angel came down to the beach, a blanket around her pajamas.

I laughed. "I'm breaking some rules, Angel. Turning into a moth." I walked out into the water then, keeping my back to the waves, deeper and deeper, until I was up to my chest. Water is different at night. Better. Softer and more mysterious. I plunged under and rose up.

"Look!" Angel cried, pointing at me.

I looked down. My shoulders streamed with green glowing water, and two neon rivers poured off my arms. When I spun around to see behind me, my hair sprayed an arc of emeralds.

"Oh, my father told me about this!" Angel ran down to the water's edge. "Once in a while, when the water's warm enough, this phosphorescent plankton rides in on the Gulf Stream." She stepped out of her pajamas and walked in a few feet, bending over to ripple her arms through the water, which lit up as though electric.

Angel came out as far as her waist, and I came in to meet her. The water glowed on our bodies and ran from us like liquid fireflies as we splashed. It was enough to make me wonder about everything I'd thought was true—I'd let go of my rules, and here we were, glowing in the ocean! If Angel and I could glow, what else could we do? Beside us, the waves flashed as they hit the jetty.

"Angel," I said. "Take a deep breath and fill your lungs, then fall back. I'll catch you. Fall back."

"I can't," Angel said.

"You can. I'll catch you."

"You swear?"

"I swear."

Angel fell back and I caught her shoulders. "Now arms out, and relax. You're floating." Gradually, I pulled away until I was supporting her with only one finger under each shoulder blade. And then I let go. "Swimming lesson number one. Gold star."

Afterward, we climbed onto the jetty. Angel was quiet

for a while, wringing the seawater from her hair, facing the horizon, where the moon lit a silver path.

I knew what she was thinking about. "I think your father was a hero," I said. "He made sure everyone else was safe."

She turned back to me, wiping something from her eyes. "He couldn't swim. He died less than a mile from shore. He could probably see it. It was September, the water was warm, he should have been fine. Except he couldn't swim. So stupid!"

"But he was a fisherman."

"Portuguese fishermen don't learn. It's a *fado* thing—if you fall overboard, it's your destiny to drown."

"I guess you're right," I said after a long moment. "I guess I can't understand *fado*."

Angel was quiet for a long moment also. "Maybe I don't understand it, either."

CHAPTER

· 27 ·

Saturday morning, as if she'd been doing it all along, my mother called. I took the phone over to the window where I could watch the renters packing up. "Where are you?"

"Mexico! There's some new turquoise turning up. It's going to make some amazing jewelry. I'll send you a bracelet."

"You could just bring it when you come here. Soon, because school will start—"

I heard my mother cover the phone and laugh with someone, music in the background. She came back. "Hold on, hold on. Didn't Louise tell you? She was supposed to talk to you when school got out."

"We've been busy. With the cottages. It's not hard work, though! Tell me what?"

"Put her on, Stella."

"I can't." I glanced over to the garden. "She's . . . in the garden. Tell me what?"

I heard my mother pull the phone away again, cover it to talk to someone before coming back. "About you maybe staying a little longer."

My heart stuttered. The world went silent. Katie ran out of Sandpiper then, waving a piece of toast. Right behind her came her mother. She scooped her up and hugged her tight. Since the storm Thursday, I'd noticed she had barely let Katie out of her arms.

"But the court, Mom," I said. "You're supposed to get a job here. Those classes."

"I know. And I will. But it's so amazing here. I wish you could see it. Maybe when I get some money together, you can come for a visit, baby!"

"I'm not a baby! And, no, you have to come here. Now, Mom. Please."

"I can't right now. I'm broke. I'm working on making some money, but it's not easy, you know. Look, I have to go. Love you."

"Don't go!" I glanced up at the Earl Grey tin. "I have

money, Mom. You *have* to come here. You can live here. Louise needs you."

"Louise," my mother sighed. "Too much water under that bridge, Stella."

"What does that even mean? What's wrong between you?"

"Oh, Stella." Without seeing her, I knew my mother was pinching the bridge of her nose, as if my question was hurting her head. "Louise and I . . . well, she just doesn't approve of me. She never has."

"Well, not anymore. Louise doesn't feel that way anymore," I replied, which at least was true. "Come now. There's a home for us here."

There was a long pause. "What do you mean, you have money?"

I looked at the Earl Gray tin again and redid Angel's math. "I could send you three hundred dollars Monday. That'd be enough to get back, right? Come back."

"Okay," she said after another long pause. "Okay."

At quarter of ten, Angel and I went over to the cottages. I sat down near her under the LINGER LONGER sign, but I didn't look at her. Not that I was feeling guilty. Just . . . confused.

All the families were outside, stuffing luggage and coolers and rafts into cars that didn't seem big enough anymore.

One by one, they came over to return their keys.

Mrs. Sandpiper gave me a hug and thanked me again for Thursday. Katie jumped into my lap and wrapped her arms around my neck until her father came over and peeled her off. "We'll be back next summer," he told her, picking her up. "You'll see her again." He turned to me. "Can we do that? Will you book us for the same two weeks next summer?"

"I'll tell Louise," I said.

Katie peered at me over her father's shoulder. "You be here next summer."

"You be good now."

"No, promise," Katie said. She pointed to the ground I was sitting on, next to the sign. "You be right *here*."

"Sure. Right here," I said, shaken by how much I wanted it to be true. I pointed over to Sandpiper. "And you'll be right there. And you'll be so much bigger then!"

Katie nodded. "And you won't be worried."

Angel shot me a triumphant look at that, but I just got up and said, "Let's get to work."

There was plenty of food in the refrigerators, but I wasn't hungry. I stashed it back at the house, along with the seventy dollars in tips. I snapped the Earl Grey tin down hard and pushed it way back on the shelf.

If I gave it to my mother, it wouldn't really be stealing,

I told myself. It was half mine anyway. And I'd pay it back by the end of summer.

This time, there wasn't much difference between Angel's cottages and mine, that's how good Angel had gotten at things. This time, though, as I stood in Sandpiper's doorway to give it a final look, the sight didn't fill me with pride.

I went back into the bathroom and took down the pieces of the sand dollar George had broken that first day and carried them over to Angel. "George told me a story about this shell one time," I started. "About it being broken."

Angel shrugged. She pointed to an SUV crunching up the driveway. "Here we go again," she said.

I put the sand dollar halves back into my pocket. "Yep. Here we go again."

The check-in went as smoothly as the changeovers. There was another Katie, and the people in Gull brought a cat, which Angel and I pretended not to notice. Once again, four sets of parents said how sorry they were to hear Louise had broken her ankle and where was the grocery store and the beach? We told them, and everybody took off.

I went up to my room with a book. I didn't read, though. I just tried to figure out what I would say to George when he got here.

"I'm going to eat again," Angel called up after an hour. "You want some?"

"Nope."

"Are you sick?"

"Um . . . maybe."

Angel left me alone after that, and finally George showed up around seven. I heard him emptying the trash bins and then knock at our front door.

I went downstairs to let him in and handed him the envelope with the zoning petition. "It's all set now."

George didn't even open the envelope. Somehow, I felt a little let down by that. Maybe a little irritated, even.

Angel walked out then, eating a bowl of ravioli. "Leftovers," she said. "Louise is a good cook."

And George didn't ask where Louise was, as though he trusted us now. That irritated me even more, which was crazy.

"I brought the pane for that window. You did the right thing with it, Stella," he said. Which, again, made me a little mad. Maybe I *was* sick.

"My mother called today," I said. "She's coming back, and as soon as she has a job, I can live with her. She just needs a job."

George smiled at me. "That's great news. You must be really happy. I know Louise will miss you, though. Well, I'd better get to that window. It's not going to repair itself, you know." Then something caught his eye over my shoulder. He walked over and leaned into the den. "Hey, where's the rug?" he asked. "Room looks empty without it."

"She's having it cleaned," I said right away. Angel pointed her fork at me in warning, but she didn't need to—I wasn't going into idiot blabber mode. I had become a smooth liar.

And that irritated me, too.

I wished George hadn't mentioned that braided rug. Truth was, I was glad it was buried with Louise—I'd never liked it, because it reminded me of home. Not home in a good way, but "home"—the word I used to use when I was little to mean the space under the kitchen table in my grandmother's house.

I'd go there when my mother got that look that meant she was getting ready to leave. I'd sit under the table, safe between the four wooden legs that never moved, watching my mother's legs, which never *stopped* moving. She paced the kitchen, back and forth, and it made me think of the lion at the Franklin Park Zoo, where my grandmother used to take me for a treat. That lion circled his cage over and over and over again—he never stopped. It was as if he thought that if he paced enough times, an opening would suddenly appear. I never liked to watch that lion. I would always run to the penguins or the monkeys, because I knew someday that lion was going to realize there was *never* going to be a way out. And I didn't want to be there when he did.

There had been a braided rug a lot like Louise's under our kitchen table. I would weave my fingers into the loops and hold on, watching my mother's cigarette ashes drift down. I'd hold my breath and dig my fingers deeper into the braids when a cinder would glow on the floor, wondering if the house was going to catch fire. My grandmother's kitchen floor was speckled all over with tiny black pinholes.

Sometimes my mother would give a little yelp of surprise when the cigarette burned down to her fingertips, as if she'd forgotten she was holding it. Or sometimes the phone would ring, or sometimes I'd get brave and come out and touch her arm, or sometimes my grandmother would come home from work. There'd be a second when my mother didn't seem to know where she was. Then a worse moment—when it came back to her.

I always figured that lion at the zoo would wear that look one day, when he figured out he was stuck in that cage forever.

I went to my room and got into bed. Over and over, I tried to play my movie, the one where my mother walks into Louise's kitchen and is peaceful, and thinks how lucky she is to have me for a daughter. But a different scene kept playing on my screen: my mother, pacing across my grandmother's kitchen floor like the lion in the Franklin Park

Zoo. I dozed and woke, dozed and woke. And every time, there was my mother, pacing.

The clock beside my bed said five fifteen. I knew what I had to do. I'd known it for four weeks.

CHAPTER

28

Angel lay sprawled across the bed in a jumble of sheets and strewn clothes. I was going to miss her so much. A few weeks ago I would never have believed I could feel that way, but a few weeks ago was a different lifetime.

I touched her shoulder.

Angel groaned and twisted around to squint at me through her tangle of hair.

I held out her backpack and the money from the Earl Grey tin. "I called."

Angel stared at me, not understanding. And then

understanding. She fished yesterday's cutoffs and T-shirt from the end of the bed and yanked them on over her pajamas, slid into her flip-flops. She grabbed her backpack and the money and then she hugged me. I closed my eyes, but I heard her clattering down the stairs, and the door banging shut, and then the house was silent.

I sank to her bed and I thought about sirens.

I'd asked the 911 dispatcher to tell the police not to use them, because everyone in the cottages was still asleep. But I didn't want to hear them either. Sirens sound different when you know they are coming for you. Three months ago, on that cold afternoon in April, I had crouched under the table in our little apartment while sirens came closer and closer. Like a little kid again.

I knew they were coming for me, because I was the one who had called.

Now, even though all the Heloise in me ached to make the bed and fold up Angel's clothes, I sat perfectly still on the tangle of her sheets and thought about sirens, and I finally realized what they sound like: They wail like my father's trombone. Which is the sound of someone getting ready to leave you for good. My chest tightened until it hurt to breathe.

I went downstairs and let them in.

*　*　*

I used to watch a lot of cop shows. Before that time in April. I loved that no matter how big a mess there was at the start of the show, an hour later the police had sorted everything out, so you could see what was what, nice and tidy. On television, you always knew who was in charge, and things went along smoothly in order. Now I realized that whoever wrote those shows had never actually been at a police investigation.

The first people in the door were two patrol officers with squawking radios. One was a woman with short red hair who said, "Officer Meg. Are you okay?" The second was a guy with a shaved head who didn't look old enough to be wearing a uniform that serious. He asked me if I was all right, too, and he scanned the room with his hand on his gun as if he expected it to be full of dangerous criminals.

We didn't get very far because another policeman in another cruiser with another squawking radio came in. He said he would be the detective in charge and announced that he'd informed the state police and the Department of Children and Families, and they'd be along pretty soon, too.

Through it all, I kept saying "I'm sorry," and everybody kept ignoring me.

"Now, what have we got here?" the detective asked.

Before we could start, the front door swung open and in marched Angel. "I confess," she said, her arms raised in surrender. "Everything Stella did, I did, too. If you're arresting her, you'd better take me, too. *É o meu destino agora.* Do you want to handcuff me?"

The detective told Angel he didn't think that would be necessary, and then he took out a roll of yellow crime scene tape and asked us, "Where's the . . . ?"

I pointed to the back door. "Just past the zucchini."

The lady police officer asked Angel and me if there were any adults we wanted notified. "Someone you could have a meaningful conversation about this with," she explained. "Family? Someone you trust."

Angel asked if they could get her aunt in New Bedford. Before I could answer, there was another commotion in the driveway. I looked out the window. "Never mind," I told her. "He's here."

Just watching George get out of his green pickup eased the tightness in my chest. The officer with the shaved head met him.

"Now let me get this straight," I heard him say as they neared the house. "She's been dead for *how* long?"

Inside, George came straight over and gave me a big hug, as if he knew that was exactly what I needed him to do.

"I called you before the police," I told him. "I wanted you to know first."

"No reception at sea. I just got in. Now, you've been alone here for weeks? Is that true?"

"I'm sorry," I said. "I know we should have told you."

"You've been running this place all by yourselves since— Oh, Lord. The pumpkins?"

I nodded.

"Unbelievable," George muttered.

And just then *another* person arrived. He wore a regular suit, but you could tell he was in charge, or he expected to be. He lifted his badge to the patrol officers. "State Trooper Ellison. Crime Prevention and Control. What do you have so far?"

Officer Meg started to tell him, and the trooper took out a notebook. "Has the victim been identified?" he asked. "Do you have a suspect?"

Even though it was July, I shivered like January when I heard the words "victim" and "suspect." George put his hand on my back. Warm, heavy, and safe.

"Hold on now." George stepped up to the trooper, his hand still steady on my back. "Let's just hold on. These are young girls here. They've been running this place like grown-ups—I couldn't have done a better job myself—but they are just young girls. Let's remember that. They've got to be scared half to death. And they're good kids—really good kids—I can vouch for that. If anyone's to blame here, it's me. I shoulda known something was wrong. Shoulda known when I didn't see Louise that first weekend. Well, I did know, I guess. I knew in my gut that something was wrong. But no, I didn't want to lose a day fishing. Heck, even Treb knew, didn't he?" He turned to me. "I apologize for that. I shoulda known and I shoulda seen to things. I'm sorry."

Believe it or not, *another* car pulled in then. Three people got out, loaded down with briefcases and cameras and lights. In all the commotion, I felt like a bear coming out of his cave after a long hibernation—everything was suddenly too bright and too loud, and there was way too much stuff going on.

Officer Meg seemed to be feeling the same way. She turned to Angel and me. "Let's take this down to the station," she said. "These people have work to do."

She led us out to the cruisers. George followed. The sun was just starting to come up, and I suddenly thought of what he had said that first day after Louise had died: "Pretty day." It was going to be a pretty day.

"Are you going to be okay?" he asked.

"I'm going to be okay," I said.

"I have to stay here until . . ." He motioned toward the

garden with his shoulder. "I'll be along when I can."

The officers put us in the backseat, then got in and started up the cruiser. Angel immediately stuck her fingers through the wire partition between us and the front seat.

I leaned over and caught Angel's hand—just to stop her, because we didn't need to make things worse by committing some police cruiser crime, too. But Angel squeezed my hand and held it, looking relieved. I felt relieved, too.

"Why did you come back?" I whispered.

Angel threw up her free palm as if it had been a total shock to her, too. "I got a ride right away. Nice lady, on her way to work at a coffee shop in Dennis. She asked me if I was running away from home. And when she said it, I thought, yeah, I am. But that was so crazy—I mean, I was supposed to be running toward a home, right? I figured: My aunt has gone through so much to have me. She's sold her house, come to another country, learned how to speak English. I didn't want to mess it all up by doing something as crazy as running away from a home. So I asked the lady to take me back."

I turned around to look at the little Lucky Charms cottages, shining in the dawn's pink light like a postcard. As we drove down the road, the cottages grew smaller and smaller.

CHAPTER

◇ 29 ◇

We were separated in the police station.

I was sorry I couldn't be in two places at one time, because I would have liked to hear Angel's version. When Angel told about something, even a boring soap opera, it turned into a Something. She would probably have that police officer's mouth hanging open at how exciting our lives had been the past four weeks. She'd leave him begging to know, "And *then* what happened?"

Officer Meg led me down a hall to a small room. "This is Officer Massey, the youth officer," she introduced us. While he and Officer Meg exchanged notes, I studied the room. It was small and cluttered and had windows on only one wall. A counter ran along that wall, with a sink and a coffeemaker and a litter of cups and spoons.

And a box of doughnuts.

Now, if I were a policeman and I wanted a doughnut, I wouldn't advertise the fact—too many jokes about cops and doughnuts. I'd hide the box. But I have to say I was really glad Officer Massey hadn't. Just looking at those doughnuts made my mouth water, and I couldn't look away. Officer Massey must have noticed. He brought the Dunkin' Donuts box over to the table and nodded that I should take one. Which I did. Boston Kreme. Three bites later, it was gone. "They're nothing but air these days," he said. "Better have another." Which I did. Chocolate glazed.

Officer Massey poured himself a cup of coffee and one for Officer Meg, and then he picked up a third cup. For a second I could tell he thought about pouring me one, too, but he remembered I was just a kid. "Terrible anyway," he mumbled. "Tastes like mud."

"You should keep your coffee in the freezer," I said, with a nod to the bag on the counter. "It stays fresher that way. And your carafe has lime scale on it, on account of the minerals in the water. You should run vinegar through your machine every once in a while to take care of that."

Officer Massey stared at me as if I'd just given him the

formula for nuclear fission. "Who *are* you?" he asked.

I almost laughed, but then I told him my full name—after all, I was in a police station, hauled in for questioning. "Am I a suspect?" I asked. "Or just a 'person of interest'?"

"You're definitely a person of interest to me, Stella," Officer Massey said. "But right now, why don't you just tell me what happened." He slid the doughnut box over, and I took a cinnamon cruller. "From the beginning."

I told the story my way, the way I'd been practicing with those *Reader's Digest* books, which meant spending lots of time on the cleaning-up parts, and the people-getting-to-know-each-other parts.

"Do you know what it takes to turn over four cottages in five hours?" I asked. "To make them all clean and welcoming, down to fresh flowers, which I think makes people feel special on their vacation?"

"No, I don't," said Officer Massey. He had his pencil ready to go. "Why don't you tell us."

So I did. And when I was through, I told about the other thing.

"You got to know her? After she was . . . deceased?"

"We did. We found out a lot about her. She was a real Yankee, but she was nice underneath. Angel and I were lucky."

It took a long time. The officers asked a hundred

questions I didn't think had anything to do with anything, and then a few that did.

"What made you so certain she was dead?" Officer Meg asked.

I considered that for a long time. First, of course, there had been the sight of her. When I described it, Officer Massey looked at me in sympathy, as if he'd seen that before and he knew how awful it must have been. "She was cold, too, and stiff," I added. "And she hadn't gotten to her second cup of coffee, which I'd never seen before. But that wasn't it."

"What was it then, Stella?" he asked kindly. "What made you so sure?"

"It was just that . . ." I hesitated, and then I said it. "I always know when someone's left me. And when I saw her, I knew she'd gone away."

He asked me the hardest question next. "Why didn't you call us when you found her?"

I paused to sort through all the reasons. None of them seemed right anymore. "Do you know that the world spins at a thousand miles an hour?" I asked him finally. "I guess I just needed to fall down and clutch hold for a while."

Finally, after about another hundred questions, the officer with the shaved head stuck his head in and motioned for Officer Meg. When she came back, she said, "Well, I think that wraps it up here."

I followed her into a bigger meeting room, which I have to say wasn't any neater, and sat down at a big table. Angel was already there, and George, and Mrs. Marino.

Officer Massey joined us in a few minutes. "All right," he said, laying a stack of papers on the table. "It's pretty clear there wasn't a crime committed here. We're all agreed on that." He stopped to give Angel and me stern looks. "Not that you acted well. You should have called right away. You both made a lot of bad judgments."

Angel and I nodded. He didn't have to tell us that.

"The situation as I understand it is just an improper burial," he said to Mrs. Marino. "But until the autopsy confirms their story of the death, the girls are going to need to have temporary secure custody. Can you give me that?"

"Of course," said Mrs. Marino.

Officer Massey left to start the paperwork, and I asked what that meant. "Secure custody? Are we going to jail?"

"Not at all," she answered. "It just means that whoever takes care of you will have to promise to keep you from running."

Just then, the door swung open and a short, red-faced woman burst into the room. A long black braid, streaked with silver, whipped around behind her.

"Angelina Maria!" she cried, spying Angel. *"Ô Jesus querido!"*

Angel jumped up and knocked over her chair. *"Tia Maria-Jose?"*

Angel's aunt crossed the room and swept Angel into a tight hug. They spoke together in Portuguese for a minute; then Angel looked up at Mrs. Marino. "She wants to take me now. Can I go?"

Mrs. Marino stood up. "I'm glad you could get here, Ms. Tomé. Angel could use some family support right now. But as I explained on the phone—"

Angel's aunt responded with a string of Portuguese. I couldn't understand a word, but I wouldn't have wanted to be Mrs. Marino just then.

"Tia Maria-Jose, no, no, no," Angel tried to calm her aunt down. "Louise was *alive* when they sent me there!"

Angel's aunt brushed the words away. She stood behind Angel, one arm crossed over Angel's chest like armor, and faced Mrs. Marino.

Mrs. Marino walked over to her. "Ms. Tomé, we understand your position. Unfortunately, the situation hasn't changed. You'll still need proof of employment and habitation we verify as suitable before we can turn Angel over to you."

I remembered what Angel had said about how much her aunt had gone through to get here. Whatever it took, she did it, because taking care of Angel was her destiny.

And it came to me. No matter how I looked at it, it was the answer. I went over to George and whispered in his ear.

He looked at me hopefully, as if he really wanted to believe the solution was that simple.

"Really," I said. "I taught her everything."

George shot me a private thumbs-up and walked over to the arguing women. "Are you saying this woman just needs a job?" he interrupted. "She needs a job and a decent home, and then you're saying this girl can live with her aunt?"

"Our policies are in the best interests of the children," Mrs. Marino said. She was looking kind of frazzled. She turned back to Angel's aunt. "I'm sure you can understand—"

"Well, I could use someone."

At first, they didn't pay George any attention, because Angel's aunt was still busy letting Mrs. Marino have it.

George put his hand on Angel's shoulder. "I could use someone," he repeated. "I've got a cottage colony to run, and it's the middle of the season and I'm still shorthanded on the boat. Stella says you know how to do everything, and you could show your aunt. . . . Could you ask her?"

Angel looked over at me, surprised. I nodded yes.

And then Mrs. Marino got the picture. "Are you offering Ms. Tomé a job?"

"I am. With a place to live."

"Is this a full-time position?"

"Let's call it a trial period for now, but if it works out, yes. She gets a place to live in exchange for managing the cottages. Louise had disability to supplement. This woman will have to pick up some extra work, but yep, if it works out, the position is full-time. And it starts today. So you let this girl go home with her aunt now."

"Well, if you'll offer that job formally, and document the terms of occupancy, I think the state would be very happy with that resolution. We've already cleared Ms. Tomé, and we've obviously approved the home, so if she'll just guarantee her niece's whereabouts . . . Very happy indeed."

It took a few minutes, but Angel was able to explain it to her aunt, and from the way that woman hugged George, I could see that she was pretty happy with the resolution, too. "*Obrigada,* thank you, *obrigada!*" she cried over and over again.

The dispatcher led Angel and her aunt over to a desk and handed out some papers. Angel turned back to me and raised her hand.

I gave her a wave back, but it stung. My jealous heart was cramping up. Angel was going home. To the place I really wanted to be mine. To the place that felt like mine already.

Suddenly George was back. He crouched down next to me.

"Is everything okay at the cottages?" I asked.

"Everything's fine. Under control."

I thought about the scene in the house when we'd left, then tried to imagine what might be going on in the garden. "I guess we ruined the renters' vacations," I whispered.

"Naw," George said. "You just gave 'em something to talk about when they get home."

"I'm so sorry. We should have told you. I know Louise was your friend."

He gave me a quick smile, but then his eyes filled with tears. I looked down at my lap, because I hated seeing how much misery I'd brought him. But he put his hand on my chin and turned my face to his. "I know you're going to be with your mother soon, and I know you're excited about that. I'm happy for you. I just want to tell you that I'm going to miss you."

I nodded and looked away again, ashamed of how much lying I'd done. When he left, I couldn't watch.

Mrs. Marino touched my elbow. "We can leave, too, Stella."

"Where? My mother . . . ?"

"We located her. You'll see her soon. But you know

there are still the court's requirements. It will still be a while before we can get the two of you back together."

Mrs. Marino saw me remembering who'd made the call that had put up all these roadblocks. "You did the right thing, Stella. There's no question."

"Who does that to her own mother?" I whispered. The first time I'd said that sentence out loud.

"Someone who knows what's right. A child who knew she shouldn't have been left alone." Mrs. Marino sounded sure of herself. "For now, you'll go back to the Juvenile Diversion Center. Where you were before you came to Louise's."

I guess I didn't hide my feelings very well.

Mrs. Marino squeezed my shoulder. "It was only a short wait last time, remember?"

Except that last time I had a relative who wanted to take me in. And last time I didn't have a history of burying the people who gave me a home. I was going to be at the Juvenile Diversion Center until my mother got it together. And that might be a long, long time.

I saw Angel one more time that day, when I went back to Louise's to pack my stuff. As we pulled into the driveway, I turned my head away from the cottages. And I didn't even look in the direction of the backyard. I couldn't have borne seeing the torn-up earth, or the bushes I knew were going to die now.

I went straight to my room and bent down to give the little iron dog a final pat. "Stay," I told him. "You stay." And then I packed my suitcase.

After I finished, I went to Angel's room. "Here," I said. "This is for you. There are a lot of tips in it that will help you run things here." I handed her my file of Hints from Heloise clippings.

"But . . . ?"

I shook my head. "I don't need it anymore. Besides," I admitted, "I've memorized them all anyway."

"Hold on," Angel said. She rooted around in her backpack and pulled out a CD. "I was wrong. You can understand it. And anyway, I've memorized it, too."

"Thank you." I slipped *Legends of Fado* into my backpack.

CHAPTER
◇ 30 ◇

I almost didn't recognize George. He wore a suit and tie, and his hair was newly cut—you could practically still see the scissors tracks. His face glowed as if he'd just had a shave. He looked about three inches taller, too, standing next to Angel's aunt. He put his hand on her shoulder, because even though she was the only person here who had never met Louise, she was crying. I guess Angel must have told her some nice things about my great-aunt.

Angel had changed, too, in the three weeks since I'd seen her. She looked older, in a black dress, and even though she wasn't smiling, I thought she looked happy. Like she had a secret. George gave me a hug. "How have you been, Stella by Starlight? We've missed you at Linger Longer."

A stone of jealousy suddenly grew in my throat, making it impossible to answer. I looked away.

Besides Angel and her aunt, there were only maybe a dozen people around the grave. I recognized the lady who ran the diner, and the postman. The rest were older women I'd never seen before—probably Louise's bingo friends. I wondered which one was Anita.

Louise had actually been buried here a couple of weeks ago. I thought it probably suited her to be here. She would like how neat the grass looked, as if it had just been vacuumed, and she'd approve of the trees and shrubs and pots of flowers all around.

The minister called us to gather at the grave. He said a prayer, and then he talked about life being a gift that isn't supposed to last forever. "That's what makes it so precious," he said. The pastor had said that at my grandmother's service, too—as if that would be a comfort to anyone. Then he asked for people to share a thought about the deceased.

George stepped forward. He looked around at all of us and smiled. "When Louise got the news about her heart last year, she asked me not to tell anyone. Said there wasn't anything to be done about it, so what's the point in having people feel sorry for her? I suggested she might want to quit doing the cottages, take it easy. She said no, that it brought her pleasure to take care of them, like her gardening. A while later, she told me she was going to take in her great-niece, and then another girl. I thought maybe she was a little crazy—all that extra work and worry at her age. But she said if she only had a few years left, she didn't want to spend them alone. And she might as well do something good, make a difference in the world." George looked over at Angel and me. "I think anyone who knows these two young ladies here would agree that she did exactly that." Then he gestured for Angel to come up beside him.

Angel stepped forward. She looked down at the ground and settled a piece of black lace over her shoulders. She stood there for a while, her head hanging low. I began to be worried for her—of all people, Angel being shy about speaking. The people around the grave site looked around at the trees and cleared their throats.

And then Angel took in a deep breath of air, so deep I could see her shoulders rise. She lifted her head and opened her mouth. And she sang.

The notes poured out like violin music: sad and aching and sweet at the same time. I recognized the voice—it was the one I had heard floating out of her room at Louise's that one afternoon. And now, even though I still couldn't understand the words, I knew what they meant. Angel's song was about all the things I had lost in my life and all the things I would never have; about the things we had all lost and would never have. And while it was mournful, it was joyful, too, because she sang that we would all have so much more. Her song was about the things that connected us all.

My heart swelled with the notes, and it rose in my chest. The music flooded through my cramped-up heart and burst out in tears, hot and wet on my cheeks.

Two years was a long time to hold back tears. I cried through Angel's song, and when she was finished, I raised my thumbs to let her know her fado performance had been a success.

Then it was my turn. George took my elbow and guided me forward.

The tears were still coming, but I didn't care. "Louise prepared for things," I said. I took an extra breath and steadied my voice. "Louise prepared for things. She thought ahead about what people would need, and she made sure she was ready. And not just people, actually. She planted peas and beans, and she had trellises ready for them to climb. She saved coffee grounds for her blueberry bushes, because they love acid. That says a lot about someone.

"But the best preparation she did was for Angel and me. Somehow, she figured out ahead of time what we would need. She took us in and she said, These girls will need what's here: my home, the cottages, George. And each other. Louise knew that Angel and I needed each other.

"I wish I could thank her for that."

Everyone gathered back at the house. It made me happy to see that nothing had changed. The kitchen was clean and shiny, the way Louise used to keep it. Platters of pastries sat on the kitchen table, and more were cooling on the stove.

"*Malasadas*—they're like doughnuts," Angel said, pointing out the different kinds. "This is sweet bread and these are *pastéis de nata*—egg custard tarts. My aunt loves Cape Cod. She says it reminds her of the Azores. She bakes all the time. She sells to the diner, and people are going crazy for them. Oh, and guess what else she does?"

Angel opened the freezer and pointed to a tinfoil package nestled next to Louise's coffee cake. "I'm not kidding. . . . In case someone stops by unexpectedly."

I laughed at that and gave Angel's aunt a wave across the room.

Then Angel pulled out our Earl Grey tin. "We had three hundred twenty-four dollars at the end," she said.

"I forgot," I said. "That's a lot of money."

"Half of that is yours. Do you want it?"

"What about your mother's guitar?"

Angel shook her head. "I'm going to leave it the way it is. It tells a story this way."

I felt a sudden happiness fill me, warm and heavy, knowing that George had been talking to Angel.

"I was thinking that we earned it together," Angel said. "So maybe we should spend it together, too."

"That sounds good. Do you have any ideas?"

"I want to buy George an extra survival suit. I've been putting the cleaning tips in these past three weeks, and also my babysitting money. There's over five hundred dollars now. But if you have a different idea . . ."

"That's what I want to do with it," I said. "That's it exactly."

Then Angel asked me how things were for me. "Are you in a new place?"

I shook my head. "I go home with Mrs. Marino on weekends, though."

"What about your mother?" Angel asked.

"She came back," I said. "I saw her. She started taking landscaping design classes at the community college. But . . . she's in Florida now, I think."

Lately, I'd been thinking a lot about the Christmas ornament my grandmother had compared her to. About how hard it would be if you couldn't bounce when life dropped you. "She's trying," I said.

I left Angel there then and went out the kitchen door. I'd been dreading seeing Louise's garden, afraid of the wild tangle of weeds it might have become, with the vegetables shriveling up and dying. But it looked wonderful. Where we'd buried her—where they'd dug her up, too—was now planted with chrysanthemums, the kind you see in pots in the grocery store at the end of summer, deep red and gold. The rest of the garden was as neat as Louise would have kept it, and filled with ripe tomatoes and eggplants and peppers, so I guessed Angel's aunt was a gardener. I kept my gaze away from the cottages as I stepped over the fencing and into the back area.

I gasped. Every blueberry bush was covered with brown webs, as if all the branches were wearing mittens. At first I figured they were nests of eggs—that the gypsy moths were using my bushes as their nursery. I ran over to the nearest bush to tear them off. But then I saw: They weren't webs. All the branches had been netted in onion bags. Inside each bag, the stems were loaded with ripe blueberries.

Angel was beside me then. She was grinning.

I waved my hand over the bushes. "What is this?"

"Birds," she said. "They really like blueberries."

"You did this?"

Angel beamed harder. "The diner gave me probably

fifty bags, I guess, and I got the rest at the pizza place and that restaurant near the beach."

"Why, Angel? You don't even like fruit!"

"George's orders. He's the boss." Angel smiled and pointed back to the steps, where George was standing. She waved him over, and then she went back inside.

George put his arm around my shoulder and told me I'd done a good job at the cemetery. "I knew you would, a course."

We stood there in silence for a minute. I had the feeling George wanted to say something, but maybe he didn't know how to get started. I wasn't in any hurry, because I was pretty happy right where I was with George's arm around me and looking out over all these bushes I had saved. Even though Louise wasn't out here anymore, I somehow felt she was smiling with me.

After another minute, George pointed to the trunk of the oak beside me. "Look. Gypsy moth," he said. "That's the little devil that caused you so much trouble."

It blended in with the mottled brown bark, but I recognized it from all the research I'd done. "Look at those crazy big antennae," I said. "Like he's got to know everything that's going on." Then I pointed out a small cream-colored moth, nestled in the crook of a twig. "That's the female," I said. "They can't fly. They're too heavy. They lay their eggs and then they just crawl around in the same place. That's it for them."

Suddenly, I didn't want to talk about mothers who didn't go anywhere. "Is everything okay at the cottages?"

"Fine, everything's fine. It was a little hectic the first week, but Angel's aunt did a great job."

I nodded. "So the trial period worked out. Good. And now it will be permanent."

"Well, actually, no. She's not staying. Did Angel tell you that?"

I turned to look at George, surprised.

"She says it's not her destiny." He spread his hands. "You can't fight that, now can you? The diner's expanding. They're opening a bakery next door, and Maria's going to run it. There's an apartment over it. They'll live there."

"Oh. So, then, I guess you'll have to find someone for here next summer."

My heart started to clench at the thought of a stranger waking up here, walking out to this backyard. Greeting the summer families, visiting with George. All of it. But then I felt it relax. George would find the right person, someone who deserved to be here. And the right person was not my mother.

George shook his head. "It's time for me to come home," he said. "I was born here, I think I should end up here. Since my wife died, I've been fishing night and day just to avoid being alone in that house in Dennis. I hate being alone. I'm renting the house out to Johnny Baker—those twins are going to be running around pretty soon, and they'll need the space. I gave him a good deal, and in exchange, he'll captain the boat for me. I'll still fish, but only when I want to."

"On the finest-kind days," I said.

"That's right. On the finest-kind days. Otherwise I'll be here."

"But you'll be alone here," I said.

"Well, I'm hoping not, Stella by Starlight. I've got something to ask you."

George led me over to the picnic table and sat down beside me. "I called your Mrs. Marino, figured she'd know where you and your mom ended up. I wanted your address so I could drop you a note and let you know how things were going at Linger Longer, so you wouldn't worry. She told me what was going on. As soon as I heard you still needed a place to be and a foster parent, I applied. There were about a hundred forms to fill out, and a hundred tests, but I passed them all. So the only thing left is you. What do you say?"

"Do you mean live here? With you?"

George nodded. "With me and Treb."

The thing is, I need time to think about things. To think ahead about all the things that could go wrong. "I lied to you," I said. "About Louise, about her having a boyfriend, about my mother. I even lied about the braided rug that last day."

"So I learned," George said. "Which reminds me." He slid his hand into his suit jacket and pulled out a little silver-framed photo. "They found this, too. I thought you might want it."

I looked down at my grandmother and Louise, both of them younger than I was now. Louise had her arms around my grandmother. My grandmother had put her arms around me. Both of them had lived right here. Where I might live.

"Aren't you worried that I'll keep on lying?" I said— kind of quietly, since I wasn't sure I wanted George to hear the question.

"I'll take my chances. I don't think it's your nature. You weren't all that good at it, now that I look back."

"Well, what about my mother?" I asked. "What if she comes back? What if she gets a place and wants me to go there?"

"Then you'll go there."

"Well, what if she wants to visit me here?"

George shrugged. "She might."

"And then what?"

"And then she'll visit you here."

"What if she wants to leave again?"

"Then I guess she'll leave."

"And what if she wants me to go with her?"

"Then you might go with her." George stood up to face me. "I don't know what will happen. I don't know. But I can promise you this, Stella: Whatever else happens, you will have a home with me whenever you need one. Fair enough?"

I couldn't hold back anymore. I jumped up. "Yes! I'll take care of the cottages, I can cook, I can clean up—" And then I stopped. Suddenly, none of that sounded like what I wanted after all.

"No." George put his hands up. "No," he said again. "That's not how it's going to be, Stella by Starlight. You're a child still, and *that's* how it's going to be. The blueberry patch is yours, a course. You earned it. But I'm going to cook and I'm going to manage the cottages, and we're going to hire a cleaning service for the changeovers. Like Louise said—you need some taking care of, and I think I'm the one who's supposed to do it. *I* will make a home for *you*." He took a deep breath. Then he asked me, "Well?"

I looked out over the blueberry bushes George had just given me. Louise's pretty dresses were a little faded now, but they still fluttered like blossoms above them. I could almost see my mother's little-girl hands helping plant them, and Louise's rough hands tending them for twenty years. Then my hands, and George's hands, and finally Angel's hands, all saving them over and over this summer.

I walked over to the closest bush—a Northern Beauty, perfect for pie—and began to untie the onion bags. I freed branch after branch after branch, each one heavy with ripe fruit.

I crooked my finger at George to call him over.

"Well?" I said, handing him a bag. "These blueberries aren't going to pick themselves, you know."